Book Three

Through Magic and Madness

The Adventures of Eka and Christelle

Book Three

S. D. Pixley

Published by *Dreaming of Dancing Bubbles*

Published by Dreaming of Dancing Bubbles
An imprint of Shelrie Dawn's Desk, LLC
Florida, USA

Front cover image by Casey Gerber.
Book design by Lorna Reid.
Story Edit by Claire Baldwin
Copyedit by Nick Hodgson

Graphics from the following sources:
freepgnimg.com
openclipart.org
Vector-Images.com
BuySellGraphic.com

ISBN (Paperback): 979-8-9854698-0-6
ISBN (Epub): 978-0-9992608-9-0

Recap

We're back for that final moment, when all is revealed! Of course, you have to read the book for that but, hey, that's why you're here.

In case your break from Christelle and Eka's adventure has been a while, here's a little catch up.

Eka and Christelle met (or reconnected, unbeknownst to them - aren't words like that wonderful) back in Manatee Isles down in Florida. And there they discovered they had hidden, magical gifts. Unfortunately, all this had been taken away by their families, along with their memories, when they were children. I know, that's horrible. Of course, the intentions were mostly noble, keep them safe from whatever had attacked the Waker world, blah, blah, blah, but good intentions don't always lead to good results. So, Christelle was not happy with her family for making this decision for her. At least that's the story for Christelle.

In case you forgot, the Waker world is the hidden magical world Christelle and Eka were born into, full of people, called Wakers, with energy, or uliee, that allows them to work with the natural world around them in incredible ways. Flying on air, surfing on water - without a board, grow a tree home in minutes, even grow a ship out of trees.

Anyway, remember that all those Wakers, except for the cool ones of course, thought little Eka had something to do with her family's death at the hands of whatever monster had killed them, since she was the only survivor. Unfortunately, Eka's uliee (that's the Waker's energy from Gaia, which gives them the ability to work with the spirits of the natural world, in case you forgot) was different from all other Wakers' uliee after the attack, which didn't help stir rational feelings. As it turned out, her uliee was actually part Gaian (the spirit of our planet, which provides all Waker uliee), part Iridan (you remember, the spirit of a sun that came from the same universe as Lintu, our bad guy, and was hunting him). Anyway, I guess their non-logic was, if she floats, she's a witch. Sometimes people are weird, and not the fun kind of weird).

So Eka and Christelle learned all of this while developing their magic and fighting off the frustrated, lacking in magic, Nalos who just happened to be working with Lintu (the parasitic spirit from the other universe). Just when they thought they'd pulled off a miracle and won the day, Lintu showed up and Irida managed to save them all from his life draining magic.

Left with more questions than answers and no one interested in helping them, they headed off to the Hawaiian Waker community, with a minor diversion to Oregon along the way to pick up Eka's awesome grandparents (mother's side) and to leave her awesome truck and vardo behind. That's the part I'm not over yet, I loved that setup!

They made their way across the water in a cool living tree ship, getting there just in time for an age old Waker Rally to start. And the Rally prize? A secret gift from Gaia! Woot woot! Christelle was determined to confront the old Earth spirit and finally get her answers on how to defeat Lintu (after he had shredded her uliee back in Florida). Nothing, and no one, was going to get in her way.

Not really the way to win a team sport.

Meanwhile, Eka, whose gifts just weren't running right, went in search of answers to get to the bottom of what happened the night her family died. Oh, and to get away from her Hawaiian grandmother, on her father's side, who's a real jerk for inspiring the suspicion surround Eka since she was a child.

Along the way, she met Liney, a young cosmic spirit that was pulled, by accident, through a rift from that other universe with Lintu and Irida. Liney's uliee is similar to the part of Irida that Eka carries and Eka feels a connection to this similar being. Eka noticed that her uliee was morphing, as her Gaian part merged with her Iridan part. Liney is able to show Eka some cool magic they could do, like portalling and dissolving into energy.

Eventually, a dying Irida eventually super charges Eka, like Gaia had done for Christelle when she healed Christelle's shredded uliee, and Eka's magic is off the charts.

Christelle finally learned that she has to work with others. She also discovered that, with the help of some traveling Wakers, she could search out her mother for training, but also to finally see her again. Eka learned what happened to her family and that her brother may still be alive. Oh, and they win a skirmish with Lintu with the help of Christelle's upgraded uliee, Eka's new magical skills, and a weapon type device that Sema and Win had figured out how to construct from an old Waker book.

So, Christelle isn't so angry anymore, especially when she finds out where her mother might be and sets out to get some closure. Eka sets out to find further information about Lintu's entry into this world, going on anything Liney might remember, to help stop him.

And now, back to the saga of two Chill Chicks on the adventure of a lifetime.

Christelle Takes A Flight

Christelle stepped out of her bungalow, one of many on the tree airship, and surveyed the twinkling green canopy, energy bright amidst the dark night. Uliee swelled and swirled within her to the rhythm of the energy all around her. Deep connections, almost background noise at this point, was rooted deep inside her now and every breeze or mist of the ocean connected with her body, mind, and maybe even her soul. Whatever a soul might be.

Trees near her swayed within a flirty breeze and she blushed at the same moment as a yawn contorted her face. Before she could finish that face altering yawn, a creaking, high up, grabbed her attention. Way above, the cloth canopy bulged upward and the sparkling forest surrounding her floated lightly up with it. Ahead and behind her, giant sails, which connected the forest and canopy, pushed forward, challenging the pull of the upward momentum. Air spirits bounced around both, chattering excitedly at the outcome of the push and pull contest. Bets were taken.

Christelle frowned at the impossible setup. The expansive, star-blocking canopy, holding this living ship aloft in the air, and the three stories high sails, pulling them forward.

Had Wakers actually weave those canopies and sails?

That's, like, three football fields of fabric.

And what about the forest.

"It's really floating." She whispered. It was a ship like Win and Sema's boat, but with more bungalows dotted throughout the trees and denser greenery, the trees around her weaving into a world. As strange as it still sounded to her, this living world around her seemed more natural than the Asleep world ever had.

And now, with the help of the airship crew, she might find her mother. Or at least someone that could point her in the right direction. Isamea, how she loved the sound of her mother's name, had traveled on this ship a long time ago and they'd dropped her at a Nova Scotia Waker Community. It was a long shot, so much time had passed, but it was the only clue anyone had.

Off in a distant tree, two small, glowing figures distracted her. Air danced around them as they urged the little spirits up into the slightly creaking canopy and lightly flapping sails.

A smile crept across her face; she recognized the sharp, red-brown uliee of Ping and the mellower green uliee next to it, of Jason. Familiar faces were just what she needed right now. And maybe they'd seen where Eka had gone. She'd been MIA for hours and Christelle really needed to talk with her.

She briefly smiled at the unlikely pair, social butterfly Jason and stoic Ping, her old teammate in the Hawaiian Rally. She'd never would have guessed they were dating, Ping was so quiet about his life during their whole Hawaiian ordeal.

She headed toward the two air wranglers, across the clearing, and just as her stride picked up, a group of Wakers, passengers like her, bustled out of the trees then stopped and just…stared.

Don't roll your eyes.

But that was almost impossible. Two days on this incredible, floating, tree ship should've been amazing and awe-inspiring. Well, it was, when she wasn't being admired and whispered about. Just because Gaia had given her special gifts didn't make her special, all her mess-ups in Hawaii proved that. Besides, she'd been able to upgrade other Wakers' gifts as Gaia had shown her, using all this new energy. Granted, they weren't a vast source of energy, like she was, and couldn't talk with Gaia, but more Wakers were seeing the spirits around them and their gifts were now at monumental levels. So why did everyone keep singling her out?

Then the whispers started, words like 'the one' and 'like Gaia' drifted over to Christelle.

No.

Before the chittering group could approached her, because they always did, she called to the air and lifted herself, shooting up like a rocket and nearly tumbling off the air cushion. She hung for just a moment before calling up more air below her. She stared down at the shrinking group, hoping her tumble would dampen their crazy admiration.

Ugh. I can't even lift myself up without almost falling over. I'm definitely not worth worshiping. What's wrong with them?

She headed toward Ping and Jason, the air spirits crowding in as she swept closer to the duo. The swooshing and zipping sounds of the spirits had recently morphed into a song only she seemed to hear. Not even Eka noticed song or that melody soothed Christelle's irritation. When had the sounds around her, from all the spirits, turned into singing. Was it before this trip? On it? She really couldn't remember, but now she heard it all the time, faint but constant.

Doesn't make me special. Everyone has their talents.

She was just another upgraded Waker. Just here to fight with the others.

"That's *with*." She whispered into the wind.

"What?" Jason, grinning as she jumped off her air cushion, asked.

"Nothing." Christelle touched down on the dense branches, still frowning slightly. In the quiet melody of the night, Jason fed the air spirits his uliee. They danced at this feast, the air heating and rising as a result and spiraling up into the canopy. Beside him, Ping fed the spirits his own flavor of uliee, and they zig-zagged off into the sails.

"Hey, what's wrong?" Jason's smile dropped into a frown.

"People around here are acting like I'm royalty or something. Always whispering," she grumbled, "and sometimes even bowing!"

"That's only because they don't know you." Ping mumbled.

"Hey!" Christelle narrowed her gaze at him briefly, then slumped down. "But, yeah."

Jason shoulder checked Ping, then moved to sit next to her. "You can't blame them too much, you do have some pretty incredible gifts. Directly from Gaia."

Not him too.

"Lots of Wakers have super gifts now. We're all getting stronger, getting ready to fight. I'm just part of the team."

Not the leader.

Jason cocked his head for a moment, then put his arm around her. "Everyone is still a bit on edge, and all these new gifts are disconcerting. They just need to get used to you being Gaia's protege."

"I'm not her protege!"

Jason, and even Ping, raised their eyebrows.

"I'm not." She crossed her arms.

Jason laughed. "Hey, just let them have a little hero worship…"

"But…" Christelle sat up, mouth open, but Jason held up his hand.

"It'll die down, just hang in there."

She sighed. "I guess."

Not to change the subject but…

"Have either of you seen Eka?"

Ping shook his head.

"No." Jason gave her shoulders a squeeze then stood back up. "But we're finished gifting the spirits, want us to help you look?"

Ping shook his head slightly at Jason, but before Christelle could glare at him, she heard whooping above. They all stared up as a tiny, rainbow dot zipped along under the canopy, then disappeared over the edge.

"Looks like you found her." Jason smiled, giving her a hand up, then patted her on the back. "Thanks again for helping gift the spirits the other night. You were a natural."

Ping nodded slightly. Was he agreeing with a compliment for Christelle?

Jason cocked his head. "Ever thought about becoming an Airer? We could use a few more crew members."

"Me?" Christelle couldn't even think about what she was doing tomorrow, let alone joining a flying ship crew. "I really haven't thought about where I would live…"

"Well, if you ever want to, you have a spot here." He winked.

Maybe, when she'd figured out her gifts, found her mom, helped defeat Lintu…the list was long. But maybe she could think about living on a ship. Flying, or more like floating, on this ship, forest…whatever, really was a beautiful idea.

Jason winked again before Ping grabbed his hand and headed down. She never, ever, would've pictured those two together. How did Jason get Ping to utter more than two sentences?

Shaking her head, she glanced up again, the rainbow blur zipping along the edges of the canopy. Eka had been so elusive lately.

Christelle called some silver spirits again, but before she could chase the rainbow blur, hot breath slid against the back of her neck sending goosebumps skittering down her spine. A warmth spread through her, as familiar lips brushed across her shoulder. "Now that's a way better greeting." She whispered.

"Better?" Pekoi whispered back. "Do I have competition?"

Christelle spun. "No! Just those Wakers were bowing and…Oh." She slapped his shoulder as he burst into laughter. Ever since the Hawaiian Rally ended and they'd won, they'd been almost inseparable. The fact that he almost died because of one of her mistakes never left her mind but his light-hearted temperament and endless forgiveness helped ease her guilt.

"Still gullible."

"Am not." But she was, a little.

A whoosh of air swept around her ankles, then leapt up to Pekoi's shoulders, the little breeze morphing into a lemon-yellow spirit, curled around his neck.

Christelle squinted at the spirit. "Is that a…cat?"

He wiggled his brows. "Cute air spirit, huh?"

"But why?" She muttered.

He shrugged. "She likes me." He reached to the spirit and kind of stroked its head. Weirdly, his hand didn't go through it. "Think I'll call her Fluffy."

"And you're naming it?"

"Can't just call out 'hey spirit'? I can't believe I've gone my whole life without seeing spirits. This Waker upgrade is so cool."

Did Fluffy just purr?

Am I calling it Fluffy now?

"So," Pekoi grinned. "Where're you headed?"

Christelle starred at Fluffy a moment more, then nodded up toward the canopy. "Um, going to find Eka."

He swept her towards him suddenly and Eka was forgotten as his warm arms drew around her, short circuiting her brain as usual. And she stumbled, tackling him as them tumbled down as Fluffy leapt off Pekoi's shoulders. Maybe hiss-grumbling a bit. It really acted like a cat.

"That went different than I pictured." Pekoi grinned next to her, pushing her hair off her face and behind her ears.

Looking down at his face, brown skin glowing with lemon uliee, dark eyes crinkling, Christelle smiled back. He had been there for her, risked his life to help her. A burst of uliee spread through her and she leaned in, pushing her lips into his wonderfully familiar lips. And his response was always immediate.

"Get a room." Jason's light laugh interrupted their moment.

"We have one." Pekoi wiggled his brows at Jason while Christelle rolled away, heat spreading across her face. She glanced towards Jason, who picked up a discarded sweater before drifting away again, then pecked Pekoi on the cheek at his attempts to rekindle their passion.

"I really need to talk with Eka." Christelle shrug-smiled at him, squeezing his hand.

He sighed but nodded and wrapped his arms around her waist to pull her in. "Rain check?"

She nodded back, his warm skin comforting and inviting but she quickly wiggled away. She definitely never wanted an audience.

"Okay." Pekoi hopped up and offered Christelle a hand just as a wind kicked up and Fluffy swirled around him then wrapped back around his shoulders. He kissed her, Fluffy staring at her from inches away, and tapped her nose with his finger. "See you later."

She nodded, just nodded, and lingered on his assets as he chased Fluffy, who'd uncurled and sprang into the air.

"Oh, you think you're faster." His laugh danced with the spirits as he looped around Fluffy's weaving form and zipped off toward the sails at the forward edge of the ship. Fluffy floundered in the air a moment, before dissolving into pure energy and taking off after him.

Focus!

She shook her head and pulled her eyes away from his disappearing form, looking straight up in search of the rainbow blur. She'd see more of him later.

Overhead, nothing zipped around anymore, but a familiar whoop drifted downward. Grinning to herself, she floated up then raced toward the fading sound.

Speeding above the trees, the forest drifted under her, a living, flying air ship while way below them the land barely seemed to move. All of them floated on a faintly glowing oasis under the stars, trying not to be noticed.

Like her.

Luckily the Lighter on board kept any Asleep from seeing the ship. Christelle was still amazed at their unique ability to work with light to hide things from all those people in the 'normal' world. She couldn't believe she'd been part of that world before, been asleep to all this energy. Eka was right, it really was a magical place.

Christelle wove back and forth through the sky, faint bluish-green air energy running across her and trailing in an undulating pattern. Gifting uliee naturally to the world, without any thought, her whole body vibrated in rhythm with it all. This was her world, where she belonged. Maybe the road had been rocky, but that didn't matter any more. She really had a home. Her brows furrowed.

When had that happen?

Couldn't have been long. If only she could disappear into it, not stand out so much.

Christelle passed over the top edge of the overhead canopy and spotted Eka's rainbow glow laid out on the bulging middle, next to her glowing surfboard. Eka seemed so relaxed she didn't even open her eyes as Christelle swooped in.

"This is amazing." Eka whispered.

"Amazing." Christelle echoed back, dropping lightly off the air and next to Eka. So much easier to do now that she wasn't fighting against the spirits.

"You look happy." Christelle plopped down.

Eka spread her arms out on the canopy, the whole night above her, then rolled her head toward Christelle. "Absolutely." Her entire face seemed to smile. "I'm magic!"

Christelle nudge Eka. "I knew you'd do it. Just took a while to jump start your gifts, with them being so unique."

"Not the only one." Eka nudged Christelle back. "Gaia level magic is pretty amazing."

"I'm not at Gaia's level, I'm just a Waker!"

"Hey, just admiring your magic." Eka narrowed her eyes at Christelle then sat up. "What's happening?"

Christelle deflated. "I…I'm not some hero, or leader, or planet. I wish everyone would stop expecting, I don't know, great stuff. I'm just another Waker, like everyone else."

"No one said you had to be anything." Eka squeezed her arm. "You can lead or just, I don't know, grow trees, if you want. You're choice. But," Eka gave her a warm smile. "I think you'd make a great leader."

"Thanks." Christelle's smile floundered on her face. "It's just, I almost got people killed last time we went up against Lintu. I can't do that again, let people die because of my stupidity."

At the mention of their last encounter, Eka's whole body dimmed and her smile disappeared, along with the glowing board, morphing back into the tiny marble Eka had picked up somewhere on Hawaii.

"Oh Eka, I didn't mean to bring up that fight."

What's wrong with me?

Eka sighed. "I really miss her."

"Eka…" Christelle winced at the image of Eka's grandmother, Sema, disappearing into dust as Lintu drained all her uliee.

"It's not you, it's just gonna take more than two weeks." Eka inhaled deeply, holding it and staring out at the stars and sky and universe for a long moment, before exhaling.

Christelle squeezed her arm. "It took a lot for her and Win to decipher the instructions in that old book then confront him with us. If they hadn't figured all that out, I couldn't have overloaded Lintu, hurt him enough to make him run."

She smiled weakly at Christelle. "Agreed. And I'm tired of crying, so I'm trying to focus on the how heroic she was, instead of her being gone." Eka shook her head. "Who knew a book about an old Waker war would come in handy?"

Christelle nodded.

"And maybe," Eka looked at her hands, focus completely there, "if Ke is still alive, maybe I could help him. At least I have to try."

Christelle could almost feel the question of whether Ke was alive or not lingering between them and her stomach tightened. If Eka's brother was still out there, who, or maybe what, would he be. He disappeared, as a child, into a portal with Lintu decades ago. That can't have been okay for him. Would he be whole? Sane?

Next to her, Eka fidgeted. "Look, I know it's a long shot. He might be…" her voice wavered. "He might be dead, but what if he's not? What if he was lost? What if he escaped and he's been hiding, all this time, alone and afraid? I can't just quit on him." Eka wrung her hands, the movement so out of place on her. "He's all that's left of my family."

Christelle grabbed Eka's hand. "You have family. I'm here and you could always go see Win in his old Community."

Eka slumped. "I know."

Christelle took a deep breath, fighting her uncertainty. "And I've got your back."

"Really?" Eka stared at her, wide-eyed and she seemed so small in that blink-of-an-eye moment.

"Always. That's what family's for."

Eka pulled Christelle into a rare hug and squeezed. "Thanks."

" 'elcome." Christelle mumbled, buried in Eka's shoulder.

Tired of all the emotional turmoil, Christelle sat back and rerouted the conversation. "So, have you seen Liney?"

Eka fidgeted, then lay back, shaking her head. "No. I've looked but she doesn't like showing herself to others, even Wakers. I can't blame her. Most Wakers think I'm strange and are openly hostile, but with her? They'd probably attack first and wonder later."

"They would wouldn't they?" Christelle growled suddenly, fists forming. "What is wrong with them? You've proven yourself over and over. Twice we've stopped Lintu from destroying them. No, three times."

"Two and a half." Eka smiled briefly at Christelle.

Christelle dropped her fists and crossed her arms. "You know what I mean. I should go down there right now and tell them exactly why they're wrong."

"Wouldn't stop the whispers."

Fury drained from Christelle. "No. You're right." An image of raining down righteous anger on all the Wakers elicited a tiny curled up lip from Christelle. "But it would feel great."

"Completely." Eka full on grinned. "Hey, at least the whispers about you are the rock star kind. Mine are more of the sleeper agent variety."

Christelle hit Eka.

"What?"

"No way sleeper describes you, more like a chaos agent."

Eka nodded and hopped up. "I'll take it." She threw the little marble up and it morphed back into her hovering surfboard.

"That's really cool." Christelle watched Eka hop on the board, knowing her own gifts would never lead to creating things.

"I know, right? Maybe someday I won't need the marble." Eka winked at Christelle. "First one around the ship skips bathroom duty!"

"What?" Christelle called up to her friend, thinking of all the trips she'd made off ship to the surface. "There are bathrooms? Why don't I ever know these things?" And she took off after Eka.

Christelle Talks With A Child

Christelle tried to sprawl out next to Jason, but the damp moss covering the tree limbs of the ship deck soaked into her pants and sweater.

She sprang back up, swiping at her butt.

Jason laughed. "It'll dry, relax." He rolled over to show his own soaked pants.

Very slowly, she sat down again, wincing at the chilly shiver running along her back. She was already wet and cold. Too late to care now.

A few dozen feet away, a lanky, short crew member she'd met earlier, concentrated on easing uliee into the massive tree system which wove in and out of itself to form the flying ship. Slowly, new limbs emerged from the deck and weaved amongst the older wood, tightening any gaps and replacing older, decaying bits.

Watching the new growth become part of this incredible ship, her brain tried, and failed, to imagine that just two Balsa trees were responsible for all this wood.

Her body hummed with the knowledge, but her brain finally turned its back on the whole, impossible thing.

Jason laughed again. *You fight yourself too much!*

"Could you give me some thought privacy?" Christelle huffed.

He shook his head. "You really need to work on your mindspeaking if you want privacy."

She sighed. Thinking coherent conversation with anyone was tricky, she had to prepare every thought like she was speaking a foreign language. Probably what Jason, and everyone else trying to accommodate her, felt.

"I'm…"

Deep breath.

I'm trying.

I know. He nodded.

So, are we getting close?

She could control the mindspeak, see.

Almost. Jason smiled up at the stars.

Maybe a change in conversation.

"So, the community is in Nova Scotia?" She blurted out, then sagged into the branches. Mindspeaking wasn't going to be easy.

Damnit!

A laugh burst from Jason as the other crew member turned toward her at the mindyell she'd just let out and she erupted in warmth.

"Sor…" *Sorry.*

We're almost there. Jason wiped tears from his eyes.

Ignoring him, she focused on what her plan was. She was itching to get there, to see if her mother was there or had at least been through.

A burst of flapping sounded above and she yanked her head up toward one of the giant sails. A woman, a crew member whose name Christelle had lost in the sea of new names, sat in a vine-seat, rigged from the vines connecting the sail to the ship and the canopy above. The woman was trying to work on the rigging as the canopy, sails, and her chair swung violently around.

"Hey!" The woman's voice rang out. "Calm the winds!"

A tiny stream of Jason's uliee shot up next to her and spread out into the air of the sails and the bursts of wind died, leaving only a steady breeze and a stiff sail. The woman quickly grew some more vines, weaving them in and out of the sail along the tattered edges.

Christelle watched the woman repairing the damaged sails. Some things were really the same across worlds, Wakers still had to do normal stuff like maintenance. Then, when the woman finished, she wrapped herself in vines and spun down to the bottom edge of the sail.

Well, kind of normal.

All around her, the Waker crew seemed to be so in tuned to the spirits connected to the ship, they almost didn't need to guide the ships movement. The crew just seemed to think about where they wanted to go and it happened, even those that still couldn't see the spirits. How was it so easy?

"Does everything always go this smoothly with the ship?"

"No." Jason shook his head. "Sometimes the air goes winty."

"Winty?"

"Yeah." He seemed to struggle. "It rebels, kind of kicking and lashing out. But it usually only happens when we come across the wild areas."

She flashed back to Maui and the angry spirits that almost killed Yang and Pekoi. If she hadn't had Gaia's upgrade, she couldn't have cut through the water and wind to get to them. This upgrade had really helped during the Rally tasks. But she couldn't imagine, even with the upgrade, taking a ship through wind like that.

"How do you fly through it?"

"We stay far away from those spirits that aren't interested in working with us."

He could see spirits now? Christelle narrowed her eyes at him. Why hadn't she noticed his energy recently, the way it glowed deeper than normal Wakers, more like Pekoi and Ping.

"You've…your energy…"

"Spit it out." Jason raised his eyebrows.

"Your uliee is different. Stronger."

He nodded. "Ping helped me. Seems that when you healed him and upgraded him, he was able to upgrade me." Jason grinned. "It really drove him crazy that I couldn't understand what he was talking about when he swatted at the air spirits which were zipping around him."

Christelle found her brain rebelling again. Her upgrades were spreading. Wow. Would it work on everyone? Did it diminish as more of them tried to upgrade others? Could every Waker do this?

"Jason, I was…" A young girl Christelle recognized from around the ship, stood gawking at Christelle, distracting her from her questiony thoughts.

"I'm sorry, I…"

She started to back away but Jason sat up and smiled. "Hey, Irley, come on over. Christelle doesn't bite." Jason grinned at Christelle. "Well, not usually."

Christelle blushed then punched Jason.

"What!" Irley's whole body seemed to cringe. "No, I didn't think that…"

Laughter burst from Jason.

"Okay, give her a break." Couldn't he see the girl was trying to collapse into herself. Christelle smiled gently at her. "Hey Irley."

Irley's light blush deepened. "Uh, hi."

Christelle sighed. Why couldn't she just be anonymous? A person whom other Wakers got to know, not some crazy Waker celebrity with all kinds of insane assumptions. Well, too late for that. "So, Irley, are you a crew member."

The girl's head jerked up from her fascinating hands, her face beaming. "I wish! My parents are and I hope to be a Weaver like them or even a Lighter, but I'm too young right now. But maybe soon. Mom says that everyone's gifts are getting stronger and maybe if mine was I could help out. She said you're helping make our gifts stronger, like Gaia, and maybe you could…"

And just like that, her mouth closed and the blush returned. She must've remembered who her audience was.

Or maybe it was Christelle's cringe that stopped her rush of words.

"I'm sorry!" Irley cringed herself.

The small space around them seemed to press in on Christelle as no one spoke. How do you save this?

Jason swooped in. "Did you know Christelle likes to draw?"

"Drawing?"

Jason leaned in and whispered. "Something Asleep do."

"Asleep?" Irley whispered back, staring at Christelle.

How long had it been since she'd drawn, or performed, or anything from her life before? Did she miss it? So much had changed, that life seemed almost like someone else's.

Christelle leaned in, the story forming in her mind. "Not only do I draw, I used to perform in a show."

"A show?" Irley frowned, maybe at all the words she didn't know.

"Yes. Eka did too."

At Eka's name, the open curiousness of Irley shut down, and she stepped back and wrapped her arms around her stomach.

"Irely?" Jason frowned at the girl. "What's wrong?"

But Christelle knew.

"Nothing." Irley shook her head then spun around and left.

"She's afraid of Eka." Christelle stared at the retreating girl.

Before Christelle could drag the conversation into her frustration, a booming voice cut in.

"You two might want to come over, we're heading in." Christelle recognized Hep, the ship's Uon, and grinned. He may be the ship's spiritual leader but he was one of the few Wakers who talked to her like she was just another person. Oh, and there was his Santa Claus laugh and big bear hugs.

"Already?" Jason stood up and stretched. "Guess I'll get Grumpy up."

Christelle raised her eyebrows. "He'd sleep through this?"

"It's too busy for him down there. But," Jason sighed, "he needs to socialize before he ends up in some lonely cabin on a mountain with just his voice as company."

She could so picture Ping there. "Fair."

Jason headed toward his room and Christelle ran along the branches to join some Wakers viewing the rapidly approaching Nova Scotia Community over the side of the ship. Below her, uliee glowed like a fairy village in the darkness. It spread out ahead and below, a bright, colorful target.

A hand wrapped around her waist, and she instinctively leaned back, Pekoi's warmth and the smell of his lemony uliee relaxing her. "Ready." He whispered.

She furrowed her brows. "For what."

He grabbed her hand and spun her around. "To see the coolest Waker Community around." His grin burst from his face. "What'd you think I meant?"

She blushed for like the hundredth time. "Uh, the Community."

He waggled his eyebrows. "Sure."

"So, uh, you've been here before?" She zigged away from that topic.

Pekoi leaned over the railing next to her. "A few times. My parents took me through once, then I came back when I was continent hopping solo."

"Solo? I thought most Wakers traveled in groups."

"Yeah, but a few of us like to visit Asleep places. That's a solo thing." He smiled.

So much she didn't know about him.

"Woo hoo!" Eka flashed by on her glowing board. "Race ya down."

Before Christelle's 'wait!' left her lips, Pekoi whipped up some air and shot past her.

"You're on!"

"Hey!" Christelle scrambled to call up some air. Her start was more of a loop-the-loop cavalcade then a controlled jet, as she desperately sent air under her while she dropped. She definitely needed to work on her zen mind. When she finally calmed down and straightened up her path, the other two had disappeared into the night. Around her, giddy Wakers zipped down from the ship as it slowed to a hover, high above the Community.

Christelle slowly made her way down as all around her Wakers zoomed toward town, but not all of them were from her air ship. She looked right to see another ship hovering in the distance, it's energy faint, but colorful with Wakers zipping on and off it.

How had she missed a second ship?

I mean, it's enormous! Is ours that big?

She spun to look back, another shipmate zooming a hair's breath away.

"Hey!" She called out, rising up above an air highway everyone seemed to be riding.

Christelle! Pekoi's mind called her back to the moment and she dove down after the others, finding him and Eka already on the ground. Pekoi was dancing around Eka, arms in the air. "You are no match for the speed king!"

Eka, laughing, slapped his hand. "Yes you are! Of course, you had help, but I concede."

Pekoi dropped his arms, winking at Christelle. "Can't help it if you can't handle a little wind."

"Whirlwind more like it." She cocked her head and raised an eyebrow. "But all's fair."

"What is it with cheating and the two of you?" Christelle shook her head.

"Cheating?" They both gaped at her, then Pekoi draped his arm around her shoulders, guiding her into the Community. "These are tactics, not cheating."

"Exactly." Eka nodded striding next to her.

All around them little huts, at least they seemed like huts, grew out of the bedrock, topped with thatched roofs and covered in the remnants of snow. Everything seemed to have bits of snow still clinging to life. And like the tree houses, energy flowed through them and into the ground. These buildings were living stone.

"Are those homes?" Christelle pointed at the huts, her breath steaming out.

"Yeah. So different from the trees." Pekoi seemed as enchanted by them as Christelle.

The sparse landscape was dominated by rock, not trees. Solid and softly humming bedrock, unlike the almost ochestra-like forests of Florida and Hawaii.

"That is so cool." Eka ran up and placed her hand on the stone and energy actually danced with her uliee, not rejecting her.

"Eka." Christelle pointed.

Her friend smiled. "I know. Been happening a lot lately."

Eka was finding her gifts, a little more every day. Or magic, as she'd say. Christelle's whole body couldn't help but warm up in celebration.

"Oh! Was there another air ship here?" Christelle asked.

Pekoi nodded. "All traveling Communities come through here."

"All?" Christelle and Eka asked together.

"Oh," Pekoi nodded again, his rapt audience hanging on his words. "There are about five air Communities. And more than ten water Communities. They all dock over there." He pointed toward the water, ocean energy pulsing around a few gigantic, living water ships. "Even the underground travelers come through, setting up at the far end of the Community."

She remembered traveling underground inside hollow boulders, but they only ever fit a few people. Christelle couldn't imagine a whole Community traveling and living in something like that. How big would those boulders have to be? How many people could they carry? So many questions.

"We're here." Pekoi stopped them in front of another stone building, this one larger, towering over the smaller huts. Yet, it still hummed the same quiet, unimposing song as the others. Did the landscapes shape the Wakers? Would the people be as quiet as their homes?

Pekoi pushed open the door and raucous sounds slammed into them. Loud, laughing, yelling, banging sounds.

Nope, these people did not hum reflectively.

"Is the whole town in here?" Christelle grimaced.

"Pretty much, along with all the travelers." Pekoi squeezed her shoulder. "Best place in town."

"It's awesome!" Eka shouted over the noise and strode through the entrance, Pekoi almost pulling Christelle in.

Was she agreeing with Ping on something?

I will not be like Grumpy.

"That's the spirit!" Eka shouted back.

Before she could respond, Christelle's spirit froze at the sight across the room, Pekoi jerking to a stop next to her.

"What?" He asked following her gaze.

There, at the far table, sat a woman with hair as pale white as Christelle's. A Ysian. One of her mother's Community. And the woman's Uliee was off the charts for a Waker. Christelle had only seen one Ysian until now, back in Florida, and had thought he was just unusual. But the stories of their uliee being like normal uliee on steroids must be true. Maybe that's why they had such a fierce, warrior reputation. Their elusiveness probably helped that reputation.

She couldn't believe she was finally standing across the room from another Ysian. Maybe even someone who knew her mother and where she was.

The woman huddled in conversation with two other Wakers.

"This is great! A lead." Pekoi's voice startled her and she finally breathed. Because she'd forgotten to breath, there for a moment.

Once again, Pekoi was dragging her forward, but her dazed mind spun around too many thoughts, not really focused on moving.

Would this woman know her mom? Where her mom was? Would she even talk with her?

She stopped at the table and everyone sitting at it turned. The Ysian stared, her brow furrowed for only a moment before surprise ran across her face. "You're Isamea's daughter!"

Christelle mumbled something close to yes, kind of nodding.

"Could we sit?" Pekoi asked and the woman gestured to the free chairs.

"Yes, please." She smiled broadly and seemed happy to see Christelle. "I'm Soveil."

Why couldn't Christelle talk? What was wrong with her voice? Her mind?

"This is Christelle and I'm Pekoi and I'm guessing your Ysian."

Soveil nodded. "I'm helping to train in the Communities, but I was with Isamea yesterday. She didn't mention anything about you coming here."

Christelle's voice burned back into her. "She's here?" She looked around, trying to find the signature hair on anyone else.

"No, she left yesterday for Ireland. She thought she had a lead on the creature attacking our Communities."

The table grew quite at the last words but Christelle's stomach sank for another reason. How could she be so close? To miss her by a day?

Pekoi nudged her and she snapped out of the thoughts, to find the Ysian almost examining her.

Why is she staring at me?

"You just look so like you mother."

"Really?"

"Hmm-hm." Soveil nodded.

"So," Christelle rubbed her eyes and turned the conversation, "why Europe?"

"Well," Soveil leaned in, "there's a strange story going around, that this thing may have started in Europe, created during a horrible disaster the Asleep took as natural. Of course, it was during one of the their big wars, so they were distracted." She seemed to growl out the last bit. "There's also rumor that a Waker witnessed all this, back then. We are checking out all events that seemed like natural disasters."

"Lintu came through in Europe?" Christelle mumbled to herself.

"What?"

Christelle shook her head. "So she's going to see if…?"

"If there's anything she can find out at these attack sites that can help us fight that thing."

Christelle's stomach turned as she thought of the Communities that had been attacked, she knew that Lintu rarely left anything but piles of ash. Ash that used to be people, animals, plants, life.

Thankfully, Soveil cut into her thoughts. "We've also been told there's hope of a weapon in the Hawaiian Community, some device they're working on. But right now, the attacks are ramping up to the point that Asleep communities are noticing, so we need to work quick, try and glean something from those sites. I hate to say we're getting a bit desperate. I'm not sure how all this would play out if Asleep learned what was happening."

Christelle remembered the device and grimaced. Yang and Eiriol had really grown close since they were Christelle's teammates in the Rally and had decided to travel around, helping other Communities learn how to reproduce the devices, as responsible as ever. Meanwhile, she was supposed to travel around to help boost Wakers' uliee in the Communities and show them how to charge the device to use during an attack. But she'd been too busy with her own journey of finding her mother to focus on that task.

"You need an upgraded Waker." Pekoi jumped in.

"A what?" Soveil frowned.

Pekoi sent a bolt of energy through the table, branches shooting out everywhere.

Soveil's eyes widened. "But you're just a Waker. How did you…?"

Pekoi grinned as he nodded to Christelle. "Gaia supercharged her uliee, now she's super charging others to use those devices."

"The device needs a battery." Christelle jumped in, trying to explain what she knew the device needed. "They're still trying to make a version of the device that's big enough to work for an attack, but it'll need an enormous battery. And normally, Wakers can't produce that much energy. So Gaia needs us to…" she glanced at Pekoi, shrugged and nodded. "Upgrade."

Soveil's furrow deepened and Christelle sighed. How could she explain this…experience she'd had. The Ysian's energy was so much stronger than most Wakers, but not quite enough for what the device needed.

"Can I show you?" Christelle asked.

Her companions tensed but Soveil nodded her head and Christelle took a deep breath then stretched out her hand.

Soveil tentatively laid her hand in Christelle's, muscles tense. Christelle had no idea if she should do this with everyone, if it was safe, or if there were parameters to who could handle this and how many enhanced Wakers would be needed. But there was no manual and, as usual, Gaia was MIA. After their last conversation, she wasn't even sure Gaia would have any answers. That sent a shiver through her.

She closed her eyes, focusing on the woman's blue uliee. Why was it so faded? The energy had seemed so strong, but now, she wasn't sure.

Christelle shrugged. She really didn't know enough Ysians to understand their normal.

Just focus.

Christelle took a deep inhale, remembering when she'd stitched up Pekoi and the others. Her heart clenched and she reached for Pekoi with her free hand, squeezing tight. She'd healed them, but with every stitch of uliee, their energy had expanded, grown. She gathered her own strand of blue and shot it into Soveil. The woman's hand clenched briefly then relaxed. Nothing happened.

Christelle sent another strand of the uliee into the woman, but it couldn't wrap around the faded bit.

After an eternity, Soveil blinked, releasing Christelle's hand. Soveil stared at her, her companions frowning.

"Is this a joke?" One of them whispered.

Christelle glanced at him. "It should have worked. I don't understand." Was her upgrade fading? Or was it the Ysian's uliee? It had seemed so weak.

"Uh, yeah." Soveil shook her head. "You had us all going. Funny."

"Hey, she can do it. For most of us." Pekoi eyed the tense table. "Don't know what's wrong with you."

"Nothing's wrong with us." Soveil stood.

"Hey." Christelle stood too and pulled Pekoi toward the door. "I think I need some air."

Pekoi glared at the table a bit, then turned to Christelle and looked her over. "Are you okay?"

Actually she wasn't. Trying to share uliee with Soveil had left her with an empty, cold feeling. She practically fell through the door, releasing a breath. Had she been holding it the whole time?

"You look green." Pekoi squatted next to Christelle, crouching on her knees.

She could only nod.

"Are you weak? Do you need to rest?" Pekoi touched her face and she shook her head.

Her energy was just as strong as before, but something was wrong and she had no idea why the upgrade hadn't worked.

Eka burst through the door and slid next to them. "Hey, did you see the guy shoot beer out of his…what happened?" Eka's grin dropped into a frown. She knelt next to Christelle. "You okay?"

"No. I met a Ysian and I tried to upgrade her, but it didn't work. Something was off."

Eka glanced at Pekoi but he just shrugged.

"Well, it's a new thing you're doing, maybe there was a hiccup in the system."

Christelle remembered the empty feeling and shook her head. "I don't know, but her energy seemed weird, weak."

"Maybe some people just can't handle it."

Pekoi frowned. "Weird, Ysians are supposed to be super charged, not weak."

"Maybe she was having an off day?" Eka shrugged.

"Do you think Ysians are like that? I mean Adrien, our Ysian trainer back at Hapton's Place wasn't, but he'd been out of Ys for a while." Could some of her mom's people be weak?

No one seemed to have any reply.

Eka glanced at Pekoi again, then back at Christelle. "Did you find out about your mom? Maybe she'll know something about this."

Christelle nodded. "They said she headed to Ireland."

"Okay." Eka grinned. "To the land of butter and thunderstorms."

"What?" Christelle and Pekoi's confused question sputtered out in unison.

"Come on, you guys know that."

Christelle glanced at Pekoi, who shrugged. Christelle shook her head. "Those Ysians probably think I'm as weird as you now, telling them I could increase their energy."

"Hey." Eka shouldered Christelle. "We've always been outside-the-mainstream misfits. And, if this all falls apart, we'll just start our own Community, like the island of misfit toys."

Pekoi frowned. "The what?"

"It's an Asleep thing." Eka winked at Christelle, a grin finally creeping out.

"I guess this visit's run it's course." Pekoi nodded up. "Race ya back to the ship."

Christelle stood, nodding. "Yeah."

Eka threw her marble down, letting it roll before morphing into a board. She ran alongside for a few moments, then hopped onto the board and darted up. "See you on the ship!"

"Hey!" Pekoi's eyes twinkled as he called up air and started to lift up, but stopped short next to Christelle. "Wanna ride?"

She nodded and he swung her up. "I was gonna let her win anyway." He winked and Christelle finally laughed, her body relaxing as they zoomed up, seemingly to the stars. Hopefully the next step would be to catch up with Isamea, not chasing her Mom, always one step behind.

Eka Plays With A Marble

Eka never imagined she'd one day dock weightless next to a fabulous, floating tree ship. Yet here she was, lightly holding the rigging as she straddled her morphed-from-a-marble surf board, thousands of feet in the air. How her body and mind had become so comfortable with this was still a bit strange but crazy cool. Most Wakers she knew could ride the wind, sans board, which she had to admit had a cool factor too.

I could probably ride raw energy, right? How unbelievable would that be, not even a light breeze needed!

She patted the board and grinned. Who was she kidding, a surfboard floating in midair, no way she was passing that up.

Could she really control raw energy? Her body seemed to shout yes but her mind seemed a little confused on the subject.

She laughed at her own split perception, the laugh caught up by the air spirits gliding by. A tiny silver snake of an air spirit paused in the stream then zipped around her and landed on the hand gripping the rigging. It wrapped around her fingers, its light breeze of a body tickling her skin. The little spirit chirped to her in greeting, such a different reaction to when she'd first 'noticed' the spirits around her and they avoided her like she was a tipped over port-a-potty. They seemed okay with her now, even somehow communicated with her. Not sure when that happened. Or how. She leaned in toward it, it's bird-like chirping in her head, not her ears, and it stretched to tapped her nose, just a tickle of a touch before unwinding and diving back into the chattering, dancing stream of dartish spirits.

A flicker caught her eye and she glanced down at her arm to see the faint outline of an I'iwi bird glow to life, before its lights burst to life within her skin. It darted out of her skin and around her, the first time she'd seen it since Irida had infused her with all her remaining star energy and before she died…along with Sema.

The image of Lintu's sickening energy wrapping around Sema, then pulling out her uliee, before she could even react, flashed into Eka's mind and body. Suddenly a weight, so heavy she knew she'd never be free of it, settled so deep into her body it sunk into her bones. Tears flowed quickly and she shook violently at the pain. Sema's eyes, wide at the very last moment, were wide as if in surprise as her body disintegrated into ash. How could that have happened? How could Sema be gone in such a horrible way?

A twitter in her ear caught her attention and the little glowing bird flitted around her head. As it sang to her, the melody flowed into her body and soothed the shakes and, miraculously lifted the impossible weight in her. Eka wiped her wet cheeks as her heart grew lighter and she smiled shakily at her savior. "Your right. No more of those thoughts today."

It sang to her, like a tune far off in the distance, a comforting companion. But now, as the bird hovered outside her, the song seemed to play in her head as well as run through her body.

My song, Mele, you're incredible.

Mele ruffled it's feathers at the name she gave it, as if it were laughing. A few spirits broke from the others and circled Mele, who chortled as they spun and darted around it.

"Hey, they took a bit to get used to me too." Eka grinned slightly at the irritable warble in Mele's song as an air spirit darted behind the glowing bird and rammed it, quickly skittering away. Mele flared and expanded, it's little form morphing into a phoenix, twice the size of Eka's body and she fell back and off the board, still gripping the rigging. For a brief moment she hung there, as all the air spirits quieted, then they erupted in movement, scattering to the wind, just as her hand slid down the rigging. Luckily, her board zipped around the vines and sail, chasing her until it finally settled under her.

Mele, now back to tattoo size, settled on her arm, concerned warbling in its song.

"Holy crap, Mele." She grinned at the blurry rainbow lights and shook her slightly rope-burned hand. "That was a crazy cool phoenix impression!"

It paused, then a hint of pride weaved in with its concern. A few little breezy spirits slinked back toward them, but kept some distance.

"Hey, I think you made an impression." Eka nodded at the spirits and Mele glanced between them and Eka. Was that now curiosity dancing in it's song?

"You're call, but," she leaned in, "I'd go."

Mele chirped, a sound completely distinct from the song they shared, then she flew off into the group of waiting spirits. As the flock of spirits disappeared, Eka rose back to the underside of the canopy, shaking out her hand again, aiming for the same spot she hung out in for the last nine days. She couldn't believe they'd been traveling so long and still weren't in Ireland. They'd been lucky that the Ysian back in the Nova Scotia Community had sent word Isamea might be heading to the Irish Community but Christelle must be going crazy waiting. Waker travel definitely wasn't the fastest, even if it was a unique and beautiful ride. She glanced down at the treeship, the sun shining across the foliage as everyone asleep.

"What a lifestyle."

But was it *her* lifestyle? *Her* life?

All around her, energy of different colors swirled and moved. But, aside from Mele, no other energy was like hers. Bits of her lavender uliee, her Gaian uliee, still pulsed inside her. And Irida's bright rainbow energy flitted around. But most of it was now something else, something born of the two. A deep, deep bluish purple, like the images of space, but with bright bits of color running through it.

And she'd learned how to work more of her magic now, she could morph objects, energy, even herself into other things. Then there was the portalling. Portalling! Sure, there were so many more things to learn, but she hadn't experienced any kickback since her uliee had changed.

Yet, she still didn't feel settled. Unlike the spirits, the Wakers hadn't gotten used to her. Except for Christelle and the group from Hawaii, she was universally avoided and ignored. Except for the whispering.

"Christelle was frickin' right about the whispering." But it wasn't hero worship in the whispers when Eka passed.

Mele zipped by again, a little air dart fast on its tail. Bored with her thoughts, again, she watched them race around the sails, Mele's energy such a bright contrast to all the Gaian energy paled by the sun. Only Mele and Liney matched that deep, space energy blue of hers.

Where *was* Liney?

Eka'd looked for her everyday they'd been traveling on the ship, but nothing. Well, almost nothing. Every once in while she thought a dark blur in the distance was Liney, but it was always just an Asleep plane. And that was rare enough, as Wakers mostly avoid Asleep like the plague.

Eka grinned.

Kinda like I'm doing with Wakers.

She glanced at the sun, a sun she hadn't seen much of since she and Christelle had started out for Hawaii. The Wakers' night-centered lifestyle suited her, but everyone needed sun sometimes. And in the daytime, this living ship was all hers.

Another dark blur, but this time closer.

Closer than a plane?

As the blur raced by, she felt a melody that washed through her. Not quite the intricate song of Mele, which wove through her like a cellular hum, but more like a distracted, curious hum, vibrating against her skin.

Liney?

And then another tune, a faint sound that was all around her.

That's weird.

The possible Liney-blur disappeared and she forgot all about the music. Eka released the rigging and drifted back against the current of air, then dove toward the hint of deep energy disappearing under the ship. Her board looped but her feet never lost contact with the surface, it seemed to know her moves before her.

Rushing down the edge of the hull where tree limbs tightly intertwined, rough grayish-brown bark scraped against her fingers and emerald green energy pulsed under her palm.

Really alive. I can't believe I was so oblivious before, jees.

Then she rounded under the ship and nearly slammed into Liney's energy cloud, hazily hovering in her path. Again the board took action, banking left and around Liney, then coming to a stop. Eka climbed up from its underside and wondered if she should work on board-less rides. But a shudder seemed to ripple across the board at the thought and she patted it, silently promising to keep it with her.

"Liney!"

Eka. The soft voice floated through her mind.

Eka stared at the cloud, hovering without a visible form. Was it weird she was talking with a haze of energy, like old pals?

"Where've you been?" Eka asked.

Around all over. Too much busyness here. The haze shimmered.

Eka sighed. "Too many Wakers?"

Liney nodded.

"I get it". Even if she missed her friend, Eka couldn't blame her for steering clear of a ship of Wakers.

Liney's haze then coalesced into her Liney-form, bursting with a smile as she slammed into Eka with a giant hug. "I missed you!"

Was she hugging Liney back?

"Uh," Eka finished the hug then backed up. "I've got a great place, follow me." Her board took off before she'd finished the sentence, curving back and forth and up, way up, past the drooping sails, tight rigging, and over the edge of the taunt canopy before gently landing on the upward bulge. Then little board lay still, almost expectant.

She patted it like a puppy as Liney cannonballed into the tight canopy, bouncing a few feet away and sprawling out, propelling Eka and the board over to her spot.

You are better with your magic. Liney blurted out. *I see you sometimes from out there.* Her hand gestured across the distant sky.

"I know! I can fly and portal around with no kickback anymore!"

Why do you fly with a board? You can without it.

Suddenly, the board seemed a bit farther from Eka's hand.

Eka shrugged, eyeing her flying contraption. "I like it, but I'd like to ride without it as well." She reached for the board and her little glowing surfboard shrunk until it was a tiny, multicolored marble she shoved in her pocket. "Besides, it's easier to concentrate on the board than nothing."

Liney sat up. *Oh! When I learned I also used a focus too.*

"Really?"

Liney nodded. *My family always teaches this way.*

Wow. Others learned like her, had magic like hers. Unplanned words tumbled from her mouth. "I'd like to meet your family."

Liney nodded, a bit of storminess emanating from her. *When I find them again.*

"Oh. I'm sorry Liney." Why did she mention them? She knew Liney was hoping to travel back through a tear in space and she also knew that every Waker would try to stop Lintu from ever opening a way back into his universe. But…

"Maybe…maybe I could help you find a way home."

Liney cocked her head, questions buzzing all through her and into Eka.

"What if we find a way to portal across universes?"

Liney was quiet and intent on Eka.

Okay, what am I trying to say?

"Um, so, when Irida died, she gave me all her energy. And she was a sun, that's pretty powerful, right?" Eka's brain spun on overdrive as her thoughts coalesced. "Irida, and you, are part of that other universe. What if we can connect to it in another way, not a tear but maybe portal across to it." Away from Lintu and his wackadoo minions, of course.

I have tried, but I cannot feel home. How can you do this when you don't know it's song?

"A song, huh?" Eka paused. Was that the faint song she felt around her? Could she somehow connect to the song of another universe to find a way to it? "I don't know." Eka shook her head. "But a Waker opened that tear before, the one you came through. Maybe we can figure out how. Can you remember anything else from the night you arrived?"

Liney's shoulders sagged. *No. Just that other Waker. She ran away as soon as I came through.*

"I guess we need to find her then, see what she knows. Any information would be more than we have to go on now." Finding where that rip actually happened, based on the vague clue that it happened during an Asleep war, was going to be a herculean feat. But finding that Waker, from who knows how long ago, was going to take a miracle. She took a breath. "Let's go make a miracle happen."

What? Liney's furrowed brow reminded her of her inner monologue.

But, before she could reply, a stinging pain erupted from Eka's back, then another. She rolled down and flattened herself against the canopy as Liney dissolved into haze, agitation vibrating through her connection to

Eka. Behind Liney's dark energy, orangish-blue air spirits swirled, anger radiating off them. Mele dove through the swirling mass of pissed off spirits, expanding into the phoenix again and settling between the attackers and Eka and Liney. Spirits continued to crash into Mele, every hit stinging Eka as Mele absorbed the impact.

Eka, Liney's voice floated through her mind, *let go of your body.*

"What?"

An image, or sensation, or something, followed the words into Eka's mind and she understood in that moment how Liney became haze. And then Liney's energy surrounded her, as Eka ignored her brain and let her gut take over. And dissolved herself.

Whoa.

Before her brain caught up with her gut, a slick, sick feeling swept over her.

Then, Liney was tugging at Eka, which was weird as they were both hazes, as irate spirits suddenly zipped through them.

Mele merged with Eka as her haze floated away from the canopy, the spirits ramming her no longer having an effect on Eka now that she was energy.

Before she could marvel at that discover, Eka realized they were hovering over a scene of chaos. The sails, starting to fray and rip, grew louder as the flapping increased and the ship slid toward Earth. Well, more like dropped in spurts. Shouts rang up as Wakers woke to this wild scene.

Eka, the darkness is close. I can't stay. Fear laced Liney's voice.

What?

Eka did something that seemed like a spin to move toward the ship, but she was new at this haze thing so wasn't sure.

Liney suddenly portalled, leaving Eka hovering above a sinking ship. But she was hazy energy so floated instead of sinking with it. Her brain, though, rebelled at this weird condition and, while her gut tried to calm it down, this time it was a no go. Her brain won and she suddenly slammed together, now a solid body again, tumbling past the literally sinking ship.

Mele dove out of her arm and scrapped by her pocket, singing of boards and surfing.

My board!

The moment the marble left her pocket, it grew into the faithful little board, sweeping under Eka while Mele dove back into her bicep and Eka kissed and hugged the board. Hugging non-people never counted and she grinned until the shouts brought her back to the now of a sinking ship.

She whipped down to the deck where Christelle and Pekoi stumbled around in just-woke mode.

"What's happening?" Christelle blinked up at her.

"Don't know, but the air's pissed." Eka pointed at the sails and Christelle and Pekoi's eyes grew wide as they noticed the holes above, just as the ship pitched down again.

"They're angry, just like in Maui." Christelle whispered and Pekoi nodded.

Around them, Wakers tried to reign in the spirits and fix the sails, but nothing seemed to help.

"It's gone Winty!" One crew member yelled.

"Slip six!" Another yelled back.

Use your board.

The thought was faint, but she knew it was Liney. "Use my board?" What the hell did that mean?

"The spirits are gonna tear that sail apart. I've got to get up there!" Christelle yelled to Eka and Eka swooped down as the board expanded for Christelle to hop on next to her.

"I'll be back!" Christelle shouted over the noise.

Pekoi nodded and shouted back. "I'll find the others."

Eka and Christelle rushed upwards, the board deftly dodging air darts as they missiled at them. Through the chaos, Christelle pointed at the rigging and Eka slid them over to it.

"I saw Liney." Eka shouted over the angry buzzing air.

"Now?"

Eka nodded. "She said Lintu was nearby."

"Is she sure?"

"I don't know but I think I felt him too."

"Crap."

"Yeah. Maybe that's why they're angry."

"Great!" Christelle reached for the vines but three darts hit her hand and she missed the grab, falling off the board and down. Eka dove after her, missing as many darts as she could, but some inevitably made contact, sending shocking sensations through her and probably leaving welts.

The board shot past Christelle and caught her, Eka pushing her down flat onto it.

"Again." Christelle looked at Eka, determination across her face.

Eka nodded and they rose up to the same spot, this time Christelle grabbed the rigging and stepped over and the board shrunk to single rider size again.

As Christelle climbed the rigging a thought skittered into Eka's mind and she stared at the board. Liney had said to use it. Could she even do that? Would it get that big?

"Christelle, I've got an idea. But I have to go back down."

Christelle nodded. "I've got it this time."

"Sure?" Eka glanced at her hold on the rigging, then noticed her uliee was flowing and the air darts were zooming *around* her, every single one missing her.

"Yeah."

Eka gave a thumbs up and dove down past the sails, past the hull and under, to hover beneath the ship. "Okay, I know we can do this." Patting the board, she sent an intention into it. A slight shiver went through it as it began to expand. All around her the air shimmered and air darts scattered as the board grew under the hull till it was as large as the ship. Eka hung on to a bar she'd added underneath the board. Creaking and dropping as the ship dropped,she sent her energy flowing into the board, fighting against that bastard, gravity which was trying to drag them down further. Her board grunted, she'd swear it did, and lifted, with all it's flying board magic.

And held. They were holding the ship up!

How much longer would this work? Eka scanned underneath, at nothing but water. Off in the distance, though, a bit of land jutted up.

Managing something akin to controlled sinking, she brought them down slowly toward the water. And just before the bottom hit, she portalled herself up to the deck.

To find everyone staring up at Christelle.

Christelle stood on the rigging, singing to the air. And it was listening to her and calming down. All the orange energy, emanating agitation, was dissipating, returning to silver.

As the ship touched down, Christelle rode the air to the deck and to the shouts of Wakers all around her. Eka's sopping wet board sputtered next to her, unnoticed by all but her. She squeezed it so tight, it slipped from her and shot up. Smacking the head of a Waker.

"Hey!"

"Sorry." She laughed and caught the little marble in her hand, gently wiping water off it as she waited for Christelle's moment of glory to pass.

Christelle Sings A Song

Christelle glided down from the rigging and stepped on to a massive branch of the deck, voices ringing inside of, and outside of, her head. She pulled into herself as Wakers circled her, holding back from getting too close to them as they congratulated and thanked her.

"Not again." This time she was the one whispering.

"Christelle!" Hep's booming voice cleared some breathing room and he wrapped his arm around her very tense shoulders and guided her away from the swarm.

"That was quite a show." He grinned, releasing her as the others faded into the background. "You would make an amazing Uon of a ship!"

She shook her head till it almost flew off. "No!" When his face fell, she grimaced and touched his arm. "I'm flattered, but I…I really just want to help. Not lead."

He shrugged then clapped her back, sending her stumbling forward. "Well, glad you were here."

Where was Eka? She was part of all this. "I wasn't the only one who helped save the ship." She frowned. "Eka stopped the fall."

"That's true." He nodded, a small sigh escaping. "But you can't change opinions in a day, and they," he swept his hand over the still celebrating Wakers, "need a bit of good luck in all the glum and fear. So you're the hero my friend."

Things had been tense on the ship, news of attacks catching up to them from back in Nova Scotia. No one knew what to expect at their next stop as they headed to Ireland to search for Isamea. A little win couldn't hurt.

"Sure." She nodded, then stood straight. "But tomorrow, opinions can change a little."

Hep laughed. "I look to that tomorrow." As he turned back to the crowd, he pointed to the far side of the ship. "Seems Eka's not too worried about their reactions."

Eka sat staring at her hands with…a grin? She didn't even seem to notice the crowd shouting.

"Hey hero." Pekoi ran up to Christelle and wrapped her in his arms. "You were off the charts!"

She pushed away from him frowning. "Not from you too."

Dropping his arms, he frowned. "What happened."

Christelle shook her head. "I'm just a Waker, not some…Gaia."

"You are a wonderful Waker. And you and Eka did an amazing thing today."

He noticed! She threw her arms around him. "Yes!"

His arms carefully wrapped around her again. "You're confusing sometimes."

She stepped back, nodding back to the crowd of Wakers, who were slowly wandering away. "I thought no one else but Hep noticed Eka did anything." She touched his face. "But you did."

Pekoi smiled and glanced over at Eka. "Those two probably did too."

Ping and Jason were standing next to Eka, Jason chatting at her, his arms swinging as he explained something big. And Ping leaned down and patted Eka's back.

Patted! He might as well have swung her around in a big hug.

Christelle dragged Pekoi over to the group, Jason's eyes twinkling a bit as he swept Christelle into his own deep hug, then stepped back and looked between her and Eka. "You two are incredible!"

Christelle glanced down at Eka, head on her hand as she sat cross legged on the deck, then flopped down next to her.

"Uh, Jason, I need some help with, uh, some stuff." Above the two, Pekoi motioned to the guys and Jason nodded. Ping just shook his head and strode away, the other two straggling after.

"You okay?" Christelle asked, when it was just them.

Eka opened her hand, her marble sitting in her palm, a wet smear across it's surface. "It grew." Eka whisper-yelled. "Like wide and long enough to catch the ship. The *entire* ship."

Christelle leaned in, squinting at the marble. How could that tiny thing stretch out across the ship? She looked up at the deck, expanding to an impossible length.

And what about her. She'd sung to the air, entrancing the spirits to her rhythm, dissipating their agitation. It was almost like her spirit was singing to them. But how? She hadn't been able to do anything like that back on Maui.

Yet here they sat, two strange people in an already strange world. And Eka's gifts were so different, even more so than Christelle's. How were the two of them ever going to get away from the whispers and stares, and just be part of this world.

"Eka, do you think they'll ever accept us?" Christelle sighed.

Eka tore her gaze away from worshiping her marble, brows furrowing. "Who?"

"Them." Christelle nodded to the few Wakers still milling about on the deck.

"Um, I think they've way accepted you." She nudged Christelle. "You're kind of the hero of the moment."

"Not a hero." Christelle dropped her head into her arms.

"You know," Eka shook Christelle's shoulder, "you might just be the key to saving these people."

Christelle refused to raise her head. "That's not pressure."

"I thought you wanted to take out Lintu?"

Christelle's head shot up. "I do! But," images of Pekoi and Ping and Nani, all torn up, flashed through her mind. "I just want to play my part, not decide for others."

"Maybe some of the Ysians actually have really strong energy, like everyone gossips about. You might not stand out so much around them once we find them, wherever they are. I mean, they have to have their own Community right?"

Christelle shrugged, she had no idea except for that Gaia story of the Ysians going underwater. But was that even real or just a tall tale for the kids? And, if they found her mom or this group, any of the Ysians treat her more like one of them? Like a regular person? "Maybe."

"Christelle, Eka." Hep's voice rang out, as usual. He was waving them over to the edge of the ship where Pekoi, Jason, Ping and a few others clustered.

Christelle stretched up, shaking out a few small cramps as Eka hopped up next to her to join the group.

"Amazingly, we're right off the coast of the Irish Community and we're heading over, but I don't want too many leaving the ship until we know what's going on. You two in?"

Christelle shivered at the undercurrent of dread coming off the shore, but she nodded. She couldn't not go, what if agitated spirits attacked?

Beside her, Eka nodded as well, hands clinched.

Eka, tense? A deeper worry spread over Christelle as Hep, not wasting a minute on deliberation, whisked them all up with a sweep of air and headed toward the shore. The dark feeling permeated their group, not so much feelings of Lintu or his lackies, but lingering shadows coming off the island.

"So," Pekoi's voice caused multiple jumps, everyone spinning to stare at him. "Uh," his voice turned into a whisper. "I've heard of this Community but no one I've ever talked with seemed to know much about it. What's it like?"

Hep's shoulders relaxed a tiny bit. "Just a few families and a small Gaia source. A few of the animal Wakers live here, inviting as many of the local animals into their group as possible. It's a really secluded Community, but part of the clothes Wakers use come from here. They don't interact with other Wakers much, but we stop by and pick up clothes they send out and give them new orders. We're one of the few they'll let in."

"Don't they like other Wakers?" Eka blurted out.

"Hard for them in this world" Hep shook his head. "They're probably the most affected by Asleep on account of their feeling what all the animals around them feel."

Christelle suddenly realized she'd never met a Waker with that talent and had never considered what that meant. Everyone exchanged glances and frowns.

"And, they don't have a local lighter, another reason they've kept their distance from the Asleep."

How could they hide themselves and their gifts without a lighter getting light to fool any Asleep into seeing something normal? That didn't seem possible.

"Wow." Pekoi cocked his head "How do they keep their gifts hidden?"

Hep grinned a bit, instantly lightening the mood. "All the locals think they're some crazy group living in the past. All the Asleep pretty much stay away."

"Resourceful." Ping mumbled.

Resourceful? No doubt, but still. Having no lighter couldn't be easy, no matter what story they spun around themselves.

Agitation, like in the air spirits, seeped into Christelle. Eka nudged her and pointed down, toward the water. The water spirits, calm where their ship had landed, were roiling and breaking, growing more chaotic on the way to shore. Even the air under them trembled, the instability shaking them until they reached the cliffs along the shore and were quickly dumped, the irritable spirits retreating off shore.

She suddenly knew why. That itching, crawling feeling, the oppressive one that slunk through her whenever Lintu, or Wallace, was around, laid over this place like a blanket pulled from a sewer. And tension coursed through the shoulders, fists, and expressions of everyone around her.

"Holy turds." Eka breathed out, staring out over the landscape. Well, what was left of it. Every bit of energy was gone.

Then there was the ash, under them and floating around them.

Ash.

She scanned the landscape too, but couldn't see any signs of dark portals or shadowed haze.

"Can you feel Lintu, the others?" She whispered to Eka who shook her head. Then she realized how quiet it was.

"Where are the Wakers?" Christelle spun to Hep, who could only stare at the empty, dead space.

Eka passed her, stepping into the ashen landscape, followed by Pekoi and Ping and finally Christelle.

Bits of rock, maybe the remnant of a wall, poked out of the ground. Were these part of the homes of the people who live here?

Lived, the farthest corner of her mind corrected.

"What is it?" Hep's voice, directly behind her, startled her, and she spun, her energy instinctively growing to defend herself. He stumbled back, eyes wide.

"I'm…sorry." She held up her hands, heart and energy slowly returning to almost normal. "It's just," she turned, taking in the piles of ash scattered throughout the space, and rubbed at her eyes. "He's been here. This is…"

I can't say it.

Hep's eyes scanned the area, brow furrowed for only a moment, then something clicked and he sucked in air. He knew, they all did.

Off in the distance, a blur caught her attention. Motion, headed their way.

"Something!" She yelled and they all froze. But she knew it wasn't dangerous, just bright uliee, speeding toward their group. And, as the blur approached, figures formed. Figures with white hair.

Her hair.

"Christelle?" Eka asked, but Christelle couldn't turn away from the figures, now clearly running.

"I see." Was all she could get out.

Hep passed her, meeting the figures halfway across the wreaked and dead land. The running figures, four of them, stopped and the group spoke in whispers with Hep. Then, one jerked her head toward Christelle and she knew before the woman started toward them. She knew the face, the walk, the way the woman held herself. All the flashes of her, from the memories that were returning.

Mom.

Isamea strode up to Christelle, bearing down like a charging bull. Then stopped, just inches away, and Christelle could see the blue eyes like she used to have. They stared at one another for forever, no sound, no movement, no breath.

Then, Isamea's hand came up and touched Christelle's face and Christelle's breath caught. The soft skin and warmth, was everything she'd imagined over the years. All the times she'd thought her mom dead, then when she'd wondered where Isamea'd disappeared to. Now they were inches from each other. Isamea leaned her forehead against Christelle's and whispered. "You've grown."

"Mom." Tears, mutinied from her eyes and streamed down her face, which threatened to become a slobbering disaster. But, before Christelle could utter another word, Isamea stiffened and righted herself. "You've done well." Her mother hesitated just a brief moment, then turned away and strode back into the midst of the Ysians.

"Synstra, take samples." Isamea barked at one of the Ysians, clustered off from Christelle's group, and the woman started taking small amounts of the ash.

What just happened?

Did her mother walk away? But they'd just found each other.

"Christelle?" Pekoi asked next to her, her eyes still following Isamea.

"What!" Christelle yelled before she even realized her mouth was open.

Pekoi grimaced and stepped back.

Why am I yelling?

"I'm sorry." A sigh escaped her body and she leaned against him, both of them relaxing a bit.

Jason and Ping stepped nearer to her, Ping's arms crossed with a deep scowl directed toward her mother. Even Jason frowned, protectively close. Eka, standing slightly apart, watched the woman move with a closed expression.

"Isamea!" Synstra called out. "I sense someone here."

Christelle started at her mother's name, so real.

"Someone's alive?" Isamea followed Synstra, Eka and the others tagging along at a distance. Christelle dragged herself behind them all, stopping as the group came to the ash and wood stump of what had been a tree.

"Gaia's source." Hep's voice was so low behind her, Christelle almost didn't hear. But when she did, her heart almost stopped beating. Did Lintu get to Gaia? But wouldn't she feel that?

Synstra laid her hand next to the tree and ash flew into the air as deep earth, still pulsing and alive, exploded up, spitting a body out on the ground. A young girl.

Isamea grabbed the girl and pulled her up, a dazed look on the small face. "What happened here?"

The child's eyes blinked, but no words came out.

"She's in shock." Ping's deep voice cut through the tension and Isamea spun toward him.

Eyes narrowed on their group, ranks closing on both sides. "This is none of your business."

What's happening? Her mother, the one she'd dreamed of, was standing across from her, apparently about to lead a group of advanced Wakers against her friends.

"Wait." Before her brain caught up with her intentions, Christelle stepped between the groups, facing her mother. "Let me talk with her."

Isamea somehow tensed even more.

"Please. I can help."

Isamea's narrowed gaze held for a moment more, then she nodded, and Christelle took the girl's hand, gently pulling her away from her mother's grip. They walked away from the entire crapfest of a meeting, and out of the ashen land, the child staggering behind her. Finally finding something living, they sat on a small boulder, jutting out of the ground.

"Hi." Christelle hesitantly spoke with the girl.

Her small eyes just kept blinking.

Christelle took a deep breath and listened for any mindspeak. But, as so much of her mindspeak lately, she found her mind actually connected to the child, as if she could see the child's thoughts as little movies. Apparently, another expansion of her gifts. And in front of her, at least in this child's mind, was a hastily constructed wall.

"This is so weird." Christelle slipped through a crack in the design, into recent memories that warred for primacy, and found herself screaming as horrific images assaulted her. A faint image of a shadowy man in the village as darkness spread out from him. The Uon, the girl's mother and trainer, hiding her underground below the tree. The girl holding Gaia's source, the life force of this Community of Wakers, close. She was camouflaging it! The first lighter born to this community in forever, a child, now tasked with hiding what Lintu was looking for, while the screams of her village bombarded her hiding spot, over and over until they were each cut off. Then, a last sound before the quiet, the girl's mother's connection suddenly cut off.

Christelle ran out of that broken mind, her eyes flying open to Pekoi shaking her and Eka staring into her eyes. The shadows of the memories followed her and she couldn't quite speak.

Christelle, it's me. They're just memories. Eka's mind spoke to her, gentle against the violent shadows. *Breath, okay?*

Christelle nodded, forcing breath in, then forcing it out, focusing on the task until the shadows dispersed.

Wiping tears off her cheeks, Pekoi wrapped her in a hug while Eka sat next to the girl, Jason and Ping on the other side, seemingly standing guard.

"Her name is Brigg." Christelle said to no one in particular but the girl's head turned toward her.

The others were headed toward them and Christelle unraveled herself from Pekoi and the group. She needed to intercept them, keep them from

Brigg. "Can you sit with her?"

Eka nodded and Christelle hurried across to her mother. Her mother. Did she ever think she'd walk up to her mom again? No, she'd never even imagined it.

"She hid the source. It's still safe." Christelle cut off the Ysians. And Isamea.

Synstra nodded. "I didn't feel a source drain."

Isamea stared hard at the girl. "She'll need to come with us."

"That is a bad idea." Pekoi blurted from behind her.

"Absolutely the worst." Jason joined in.

"Again, not your business." Isamea growled.

"I have her memories." Christelle jumped in. "Everything she saw, I saw. And I can talk about it." Although, she'd rather not. "So, she could stay with Hep, on the ship."

Isamea turned her stare on Christelle, then, without warning, touched her face again. "I do think it's time you came home." A slight smile crossed her mother's face. And Christelle melted again.

"Alright." Isamea nodded.

And with that agreement, the distant woman was back, her mother kicked out. "Christelle comes with us, the girl stays. Finish the samples and get ready to leave, the air shippers can clean up." The Ysians headed down a cliff to something waiting on the shore, Christelle watching them leave.

"Are you crazy?" Jason sort of yell-asked.

She turned, Eka and Ping joining, the big, burly man walking with the small child.

"Christelle?" Pekoi's frown had never been deeper.

"I have to go." She did, right? This was the moment. And Isamea may be hard, but she saw those glimpses of her mother. Kindness, connection.

"She's an ass." Ping grumbled.

"Asshat more like it." Jason countered.

Maybe she was, but Christelle knew there was more. "I'm going."

"Are you sure?" Eka frowned.

Christelle nodded then looked at Jason and Ping. "Can you look after Brigg?"

They nodded back, Ping still holding the little girl's hand, her stare still blank.

"Then I guess we're going to Ys." Eka smiled and Pekoi agreed.

"You all are crazy." Ping muttered, heading toward the air crew on the field.

Jason looked at them. "Just…be careful. Okay?"

Christelle nodded and the three of them hurried over to the Ysian group. "We're ready."

"We?" Synestra asked.

"Pekoi and Eka are coming with me."

Isamea, waiting on the cliff for Christelle, studied each, then narrowed her eyes on Eka. "Not her."

"What!" Christelle crossed her arms. "She's with me."

"Not taking her." Isamea crossed her own arms, eyes narrowing on Christelle, then walked away.

"Hey." Eka squeezed Christelle's shoulder. "Let's talk."

Pekoi stepped away, leaving the two some privacy..

"She can't treat you like that." Christelle huffed.

"I know you need to figure out this thing with your mom. But you can't do that if you have a stand off."

Without Eka? They'd been in this since the beginning. "But, we're the two muskateers."

Eka smiled. "That's just sad. Besides, more like Laverne and Shirley."

Christelle hiccuped and nodded. "That's true. But still, they were best together."

Eka stepped closer and hugged her.

Hugged her!

"It's not forever, right? You do this and then we'll meet back up. Spend time with your Mom, maybe figure out a way we could join forces." Eka snorted but stopped when Christelle raised an eyebrow. "Besides," Eka lowered her voice, "the Ysians might have some information that could help us. They're not the easiest Wakers to get information on, I've heard they might have a lot of old knowledge. Like that book. Maybe they don't even know what they have, they seem kind of uptight and closed-minded. You could check around."

"I guess. But how will I find you?" It's not like they had social media.

"Come on." Eka raised her eyebrows. "We've got a world full of people who mindspeak."

True. If someone needed to connect, they could.

"And I think I'll check out that story. About the natural disasters in Europe being connected to Lintu arriving. Maybe something there can help as well."

Christelle stared at her friend, her best friend these past months. Her only friend at some points. "You sure. I could help with that."

Eka shook her head. "I know it's a long shot, but I still believe Ke is out there. And if he suddenly showed up like Isamea, I'd do what I could to spend time with him." Eka paused, taking a deep breath, then shook out her body.

"Eka?" Christelle laid her hand on Eka's should and got a small smile in return.

"In all seriousness, just go figure things out with your mother. It's important. And if she learned anything, chasing that crazy story about Lintu coming through in Europe, let me know. Might cut down on the possible locations."

"Okay. Promise." Christelle hugged a unusually huggy Eka then they started toward the air shippers. Christelle needed to at least say goodbye.

"Christelle." Hep motioned to a partially ashen tree where his group had gathered, one of the few living things in the whole landscape. "Can you heal it?"

"I can try." Placing a hand over the tree, she sensed a tiny spark of energy left. She'd only healed Wakers but this seemed the same. Except there was so little to work with. Uliee flowed out of her and into the few living branches and the part of the trunk still struggling for life. Finally finding the spark, she sent out a small offshoot. The beginning of a new tree, the point of Gaia's source.

Isamea, having strode over to her daughter, touched the tree then turned to her daughter. "You're...strong. Almost like..."

"Hey," Eka's voice was back, "better get going before we all join you!"

Isamea scowled at Eka, then turned to lead Christelle away.

"Don't let that house fall on you." Eka smirked as Isamea glance back.

"Eka!" Christelle slapped her arm, fighting her smile.

"What?" Eka shrugged.

"House?" The others mumbled, confusion on their faces.

Hep shook his head. "Christelle, are you sure about this?"

She nodded, for the ten millionth time. "Yes." Then moved over to Brigg. "I'm so sorry for what happened. I promise these people will keep you safe." She leaned in. "It attacked us too. If you need to talk, Eka understands." As she leaned back, She noticed a tear running down Brigg's face. Finally a sign of some kind of awareness.

"Okay, off to Ys." Christelle took a deep breath.

"Yeah." Pekoi muttered.

"Better you than me." Jason arched his brows and raised his hands.

"If you need help…" Ping didn't need to finish the thought, she knew what he meant.

She hugged them, warm Jason then stodgy Ping who actually turned away.

"He's wiping his eyes!" Eka whispered.

Ping stomped away, Brigg now in his arms.

A small laugh escaped Jason and he took off after Ping.

"Hey." Christelle looked at Eka. "Be careful, okay. And if anything happens, let me know. I can be there."

Eka nodded. "You too."

Christelle then headed to the Ysian group again, Pekoi following.

"Besides," Eka's voice called out, "what could go wrong?"

"You did not just say that." Pekoi grumbled.

"She did." Christelle looked back. "Why, Eka?"

Eka grinned as she followed the air crew back. "Why not?"

Christelle glanced at the Ysians and could think of a hundred reasons why. But, she couldn't let doubt undermine her mission, to crack open her mother's hard exterior. Ahead, Isamea scowled and barked orders and Christelle couldn't help but wonder if she might crack first.

Eka Finds An Erik

Christelle, Pekoi, and the Ysians disappeared into a weird submersible platform thing which seemed to be made of coral and Eka slumped to the ground. As it sank beneath the choppy water, all she could do was sit on the cold, damp, rocky earth.

Why was she so…blah? Scared, angry, or even depressed she could understand. But blah?

She wasn't chasing after work any more, living paycheck to paycheck, lost in a mundane world of bills and microwave meals. She'd stumbled onto a previously unfathomable world of magic, tangible (sort of) spirits, and (finally) incredible abilities.

So why was she just sitting, staring at an empty ocean? Hoping that, what?

"Christelle can do her own thing. I mean, we've only hung out for a few months, we're not attached at the hip."

Yeah, the few months in which they'd both discovered this magical world and changed forever. The months Christelle had discovered her own gifts, never gave up hope Eka would discover her own abilities too. Forgave Eka when she had abandoned her at the worst possible time.

And she was there when I had to face the truth about my family's death. Watch Sema die.

They'd stumbled through this weird and wonderful and heartbreaking new world together. Both a part of it, yet on the outside. Now she was kinda alone. Again. Would she even be able to travel with the air shippers? She'd got the feeling they'd put up with her weird magic and uliee, until now, because of Christelle's Gaia connection.

Maybe throwing the phone and bank account away when she'd learned to portal was a bit hasty.

"Pull it together." Eka mumbled to herself.

She sucked in a deep breath, arched her back, then stood up. At least she'd found her own magic. Her lips quirked up a bit. "I can get around on my own now." But, she was about to start an epic search based on a rumor about Lintu, natural disasters, and wars. Well, she knew Lintu had been here since at least she was a child so sometime before that. Her best bet to narrow down some specific areas was a library. But, she hadn't been to one in so long, not since she was a kid and Sema had taken her there thinking it would entertain her. Guess Sema and Win had snuck off to do Waker things. Unfortunately, she wasn't much of a reader and her grandparents found her, hours later, learning how to graffiti from local artists. They'd never gone back to that city.

She glanced behind her, away from the water. Hep and the air shippers were still around.

Huh. Maybe *I could hitch a ride. Can't fly, or portal, everywhere. What about sleeping?*

Her magic reserve might be pretty deep, but it wasn't endless, and she still needed to dial in everything or she might portal inside the foundation of a building.

That made her pause. Would she be okay? All kinds of scenarios ran through her mind. "Not sure and not ready to find out."

A breeze of ash brought her back to the present and she scanned the desolate Community around her, shivering. "Ireland may have libraries, but there's no way I'm staying here." Surely the air shippers could drop her off at some city with a library.

Eka stood, dew soaking the entire back side of her pants, and shrugged. She'd started with worse, and besides, a damp butt wouldn't be the reason they'd keep her off the ship.

Hep's group had gathered around an outcropping in a field, their faces were pinched in that tell tale sign of mindspeaking. One of so many things Wakers did with each other that she couldn't. Nothing came through to her except Christelle, her mind seemed to be the only one she was able to communicate with. Just another thing that set her apart from Wakers, along with her uliee, and her magic. But the biggest road block between her and integration into this new world of magic was still her past. She may have learned what happened to her family but that doesn't mean anyone else now believed she wasn't still associated with their deaths along with every other strange Waker death.

"Merlin's codpiece, this is a hard group to crack open." Eka grinned a bit at that image, then shook her head as the situation sunk in. She was kinda stuck and needed to get somewhere other than the middle of nowhere, Ireland. And Hep's group looked like the only real ride in town. So, she approached slowly, jerking to a stop at a few narrowed eyes.

Hep's head swiveled toward her and he smiled. A tiny smile, but a smile.

"Hey Hep."

He walked over to her, standing a few feet away. "Eka."

Awkward.

"Uh, so, where're you headed next?"

He eyed her briefly, glanced back at his crew for a moment and sighed. His voice, low, almost didn't reach her. "I think you know the, uh, mood about…"

"Me?" Her shoulders sagged.

This time, he sagged too then nodded. "Christelle asked that you stay with us."

A little twinge caught her brain and it stumbled. "Really?"

He nodded. "I can take you to our next stop. But that's it."

"Sounds great." She shook off her Eeyore mood and somehow found a smile.

"Okay." His voice a bit louder as he turned toward the huddled group. "Time to head back."

Murmured agreement drifted from the group and they moved toward the cliffs, Jason and Ping eventually joining them, following a few paces behind with Brigg in Ping's arms.

Ping, a kid person? Who knew?

As Ping carried her, she didn't grasp on to him but lay limp in his arms and when they passed Eka, the girl's glassy stare went through her. Eka tensed, a flash of similar eyes, her own, staring back at her from her own mirror for so many years after she left Hawaii the first time.

She let them pass, shaking out the memory before following. A shorter trip on the ship was sounding better every moment.

Eka flew next to the rigging, matching the ship's speed, the wind whipping her short hair back while the slowly setting sun still warmed her. This really was a short trip, just over night until their next stopped. Well, they'd sat on the water, making repairs until the ship was air worthy again, so she'd had a few extra nights to figure out her plan.

Ugh.

Plans were not really her thing. How was she going to find the place where Lintu might have come through? A terrible natural event during a great war? Okay, Europe was as good a place to start as any other, but holy crap, that's a lot of time to cover. And she was *not* a book person, especially history. Just the thought of reading some recount of a war made her mind want to curl up and sleep.

If only Christelle was here, she'd be way more into looking for this information. Maybe, if Liney would show up, Eka could narrow down the when and where. But so far, her new celestial partner was MIA again. And was there a Waker library? Somewhere she could look up something about who that Waker was Liney saw, when she came through the rip?

"Yeah, right. That's a really specific search. Won't have trouble finding the right female Waker with that information." Was the woman even alive, and if she was, was she working with Lintu? Way too many questions and too few clues. This wasn't going to be easy or fast, at all.

"Ugh." She knocked her head with her palm. "No more planning today."

The tiniest hint of deep blue energy flashed to the side of her and she instinctively whipped her head toward it. And wrenched her neck. "Ow. Get a grip." She rubbed her neck and the flash zipped by her other side.

Slowly turning, she scanned for the familiar lights.

Liney?

She squinted at a tiny silhouette in the rigging off the next sail. But, the uliee was a deep purple.

Calm down imagination, not her.

But who was out there?

"Only one way to find out." Excited to have a distraction from soul-sucking responsibilities, like planning how to find a universe-destroying evil and thwart it's plans, she completely focused on the trivial matter of finding out who else was hanging out in the rigging.

Her board slid back a few feet from the rigging as her legs dangled from it, then it jerked forwards, carving to the left. It carried her in a diagonal across the flowing wind, closer to the second forward rigging until the deep purple silhouette became a person. Leaning against a sail vine, a Waker she'd seen a few times sat with eyes closed.

"Hey."

His eyes flew open and he bolted up, tipping forward off the vines, and dropped.

Eka's eyes widened and she shot down after him. The tumbling figure slowed slightly below her, as wind drew under him, but he didn't seem able to catch enough to stop the plummet.

As the deck rushed up at them, Eka slid just above the slowly spinning man trying to grab him, but her fingertips only just brushed along him. There was no way she was going to reach him on the board. She'd have to try something else. Something trickier.

Focus.

In her mind, she pictured the top of the canopy, but imagined it below them just as the deck came up to meet his tumbling body.

"No!" Her body erupted in a misty, hazy, undulating energy that shot out and blanketed the spinning Waker and they…disappeared.

What…

And, as if she blinked, they were suddenly just above the canopy, just at she'd pictured, and the Waker dropped into it, bouncing harmlessly as Eka fell toward him.

She did it!

With the blink of a thought, the board slid under her, as she became solid again, and curved them upward, skimming the canopy and the Waker's hair. Then she looped around and slowed back down to the surface, hopping off the board and shoving the marble in her pocket.

Holy crap! I portalled us!

"Wooo hoooo!" Her voice spread briefly before the wind wrangled it up as it spun by.

Wide eyes stared at her as she strode up to him. "How cool was that?"

He shook the sandy blond wisps of hair out of his face. "Are you crazy?"

"Probably." Her blood pumped fast, a beat loud in her ears.

He blinked and crab-walked back from her. "You, you almost killed me."

Blood quickly slowed in her as his tone sank into her mind. "I also saved you."

"You *are* crazy."

She narrowed her eyes.

One of those, huh. Time to go back to planning.

"Planning sucks." She grumbled again, mainly to herself.

Taking a deep, deep breath, a small grin manifested across her face as her breath left her body and she cocked her head. "Nice meeting you. Seems you're pretty okay. Getting the feeling you really want to be alone." She turned and grabbed her marble, tossing it up.

"Wait!"

And catching it.

That was quick.

She slowly turned back. "Yeah?"

He circled in a crab-like walk, not seeming to want to stand. "I, uh, can you get me down?"

"Me?" She crouched down next to him, staring him in his pale gray eyes. "I might do something crazy."

"Look," he sighed, "I just need a ride."

Holding back a grin, she stood and crossed her arms. "What's wrong with your air magic."

"Magic?" He frowned a moment. "Oh, air gifts." His face sagged as the last words left him. "Don't really have much. I'm a lighter."

She hadn't met many lighters, but her Aunt Nani, back in Hawaii, seemed to have lighter gifts as well as others. But hadn't Nani just recently become a lighter?

So, if he didn't have strong air magic… "How'd you even get up in the rigging?"

He looked down at the canopy, playing with his hands. "A little air, mostly climbed."

Climbed without backup. He may be a jerk, but that's still pretty gutsy. Like something she'd do. "Alright." She reached down. "Ready?" Not expecting much of an answer, she pulled him up, his legs spread out in an intense stance.

"What's your name?"

"Erik." He muttered, eyes on his feet.

Laughter escaped her as her board elongated and hovered near them. "Come on Erik." Impersonating a freaked out rabbit, he scrambled on the board and wrapped his arms tightly around her.

"We hardly know each other." Eka squeaked at the air being squeezed out of her.

"Sorry." He mumbled, but he barely loosened any grip

She pulled his arms looser as the board moved them along the canopy. Once they finally reached the edge, they dropped like a log off a waterfall.

Was Erik screaming?

He definitely couldn't have compressed her ribs tighter.

Seconds later, Erik unwound from Eka and poured off the board to lay across the deck, heartbeat visibly strumming his neck.

Serves him right for throwing a fit.

Another laugh started in her throat, then stopped as a tiny pulse of energy flitted through Erik. Deep space energy.

She bent next to him and her fingers hovered over his wrist, where the pulse had started.

It was there, I swear I saw it.

Her own energy drifted out from her fingertips and settled on his skin. And the pulse shot through him and into her own, a hint of his essence flowing into her. An essence like hers. Faint, but similar.

What…

Erik's eyes flew open and he sat up, staring at her. He rubbed his wrist, a frown creeping into his lips and eyes. "What…what was that?"

Eka shook her head. "You're energy, there was…it was like mine."

He flew up and away from her. "I'm nothing like you!" And he stumbled back a bit, then turn and ran.

"But…" She watched him run. Did she really see that? Feel it? He seemed to feel something too. Was it because he was a lighter? She'd only really been around two lighters, but hadn't seen them work their uliee. Erik would probably avoid her now, but maybe Jason or Ping would know something.

She sped to their door and banged, knowing it was early. An eternity later, Jason, blearily rubbing his eyes, opened the door to his bungalow. His mashed up hair and sheet lined face screamed 'I just woke up'.

"Eka?"

"Hey, can I come in?"

He looked back. "Ping, company." After a moment he opened the door.

Like all the other bungalows on the ship, spaces were small, and Ping lay in the bed, sheets over his head. The image really fit his grumpy personality.

"What happened?"

Eka looked at Jason, trying to form words around the experience. "I, uh," She paced in front of him. "Do lighters have, uh, I don't know, different energy than other Wakers?"

Jason's brow furrowed. "Different?"

"Yeah, like, different than Gaia's energy?"

Jason's confused expression deepened.

"I think I saw, I don't know, energy like mine. In a lighter."

"What?" Ping's disheveled head was out of the sheets and he was wide awake. "Where?"

"In a lighter. Erik." She quickly summarized what happened. Minus the almost killing him.

Jason and Ping exchanged confused glances.

"Eka." Jason sat on the bed. "I've never heard of that. I mean, I really don't know. Lighters and electrics, they're kind of different. But, energy like yours?"

"I think you were confused." Ping stated.

Jason looked at him. "*Maybe* she's confused." Then he turned back to her. "I just don't know."

A startled yelp from a side room she hadn't known was there caught her attention as Ping jumped up and flew through the doorway.

Jason watched him, then turned back. "Brigg is staying with us and she's having trouble sleeping."

Empty eyes flashed through her mind and a sadness swept over her. "That's really great of you to take care of her."

Jason forced a small smile that faded quickly. "Listen, I can ask around, try to find something out. I mean, I haven't heard anything, but…"

"That'd be great." She glanced at the other room's door. "You guys are busy so I'll…"

Just then the outer door banged.

"Yeah." Jason walked to the door and opened it. "Hep?"

The Uon walked in and spotted Eka. "Eka, what happened with Erik? He said you knocked him off the rigging, threatened him and then tried to force your energy into him."

"What?" Eka stared at Hep, then shook her head. "It's like he wasn't even there."

"Eka, this is serious. People are already…wary of you." He stared at his hands, clasping and unclasping them. "I'm sorry Eka, but I don't think it's safe here. Maybe you should…"

"What!" This time Jason's voice rang out. "You can't kick her off the ship."

"It's for her own good." Hep sighed. "They're afraid."

"I don't care. No one's kicking her off. She's staying." Jason glared at Hep, but Hep crossed his arms, eyes unblinking.

Eka stepped between them, looking at Jason. "It's okay. I get it. People are weird sometimes." She'd been here before.

Suddenly, and quietly, Ping was next to her. "We'll go with you."

"What?" Eka and Hep echoed one another.

Jason nodded. "She's not going out there alone."

"You're crew members. You can't abandon this whole community."

"It's not a community, if it throws out members."

Uliee, from Jason and Hep pulsed, their fists clenched. Even Ping's shoulders were tense. Well, more tense then usual.

Jason and Ping were willing to abandon everything and they weren't even family. Then Christelle's words about how she was Eka's family came back to her. She may only have a few relatives that would claim her, but apparently she did have family and realized in that moment she would have done the same for them. Warmness swept over her, briefly, until Brigg's shattered world came crashing back into her memory. They had a family now, responsibilities. She couldn't be the reason they abandoned a secure life for Brigg.

"No!" All eyes turned to Eka. "No." She stated more quietly and looked at Ping. "You have Brigg now." Brigg's brittle stare came back and she shuddered. If she hadn't had Sema and Winn, where would she be now. Brigg needed them focusing on her.

"She can come with us." Jason folded his arms, still staring at Hep.

The image of Sema disintegrating flashed in her mind and tears threatened to flood her face.

Focus!

Eka needed to chase down leads to where Lintu first came through, find anything that could stop the destruction of their Communities. And maybe find some clue about Ke's possible whereabouts. That was no type of adventure for a shattered child.

"Jason, Ping. This is the best place for her. Trust me, I've been there." She looked between them. "But this isn't a place for me."

"But." Jason started.

"Please."

He stared at her for a while, then slowly nodded, a glare at Hep.

"Just, look into the lighter thing for me. Okay?"

"Fine."

Then Ping did a very un-Ping thing. He hugged her. Eyes wide, she slowly hugged him back and a little of the sadness and anxiety seeped away.

Weird times.

Before any more weirdness, like tears and drawn out goodbyes could happen, she waved and ran out the door. She raced to her room and grabbed the few things she had, then quickly surfed away from the deck of the ship. She hadn't made any plans and now she was adrift, without any clear destination.

Below her, mainland Europe spread out. She wasn't sure where exactly she was, or which country she surfed over, but somehow she'd figure out something. Night was coming, so she'd soon be able to land, making sure she was away from where any Asleep might spot her and definitely avoiding anyone filming her and posting it.

She was now more determined than ever to figure out where Lintu had started. What had really made that tear between universes possible? Had a Waker really been responsible? Maybe the one Liney saw? And how could they make sure Lintu would never be able let others like him through? And just maybe, that story would lead to Ke and what had happened to him.

But other thoughts teased her. Were there other Wakers like her? What did that mean? Her energy came from Gaia and Irida, a celestial spirit from another universe. And the only other kinda-person like her seemed to be Liney. And Liney'd been from Irida's universe. But now her assumptions were wobbling. What did that spark in Erik mean? Was it just him, or did others have it? Was she connected to lighters?

If only Christelle were here, she'd totally be into this with her. Eka's mind slipped to Christelle and she briefly wondered how her reunion with her mother was going.

Then as the night deepened and lights flickered on across the landscape below, she sighed. Guess she really was on her own. Again.

Christelle Needs A Bubble

Isamea's frown clung to her face, even as they rode along on an impossibly colorful, amazingly wonderful…something.

What is this thing?

Christelle glanced down. Hovering in a bubble of air, they rode around on some kind of platform. Which was weird on its own, but somehow the bubble stayed hovering over this thing as they glided down into the ocean.

She wasn't an expert on anything, let alone ocean life, but the platforms all the Ysians road on seemed to be made of coral with aquatic plants growing sporadically on its surface. And none of the plants, or anyone's hair, flew back even a little as they slid through the ocean, which glowed a faint greenish energy. And stranger than that, none of the Ysians were inside a bubble.

They're breathing water!

Could she do that? Did she want to breath water?

She grabbed her neck, thinking of gills and water flowing into her. A shiver went through her and the bubble seemed more and more beautiful by they minute.

Of course, the question that came next was, how stable was this bubble thing, really?

The last time she'd done something even close to this, trying to find the underwater tunnels back in Hawaii, she'd struggled to keep an air bubble tight around her, Nani, and Pekoi, instead of collapsing on them. She'd almost lost the whole crew before they'd found the tunnels and stumbled in. But here, the pressure on her bubble, as the group dove deeper, didn't even send a ripple across the transparent surface. Or phase the Ysians cutting through the water without any kind of protection.

What does the water at this depth feel like? She watched the other white-haired people from her Mom's Community ride so confidently in open water and suddenly, she desperately wanted to feel the water against her skin, like them. She held her palm against the bubble's surface. Would it break if she stuck her hand through it? Her fingers stroked the wall and a shimmer ran the length of the mostly invisible air pocket. Then a few fingertips slipped through and she froze, waiting for water to rush in. Instead, bitter cold wetness bit at her exposed skin and she jerked back.

Christelle? Pekoi's thought seeped into her head and she glanced left, where he floated in his own, invisible habitat. *What are you doing?*

She was trying to understand how she could still be completely flummoxed by this not-so-new world.

How are we floating along? These bubble things aren't even attached. How are we not crushed? Why does the air seem fresh?

He shook his head, shrugging.

You'll learn. Isamea's clipped thoughts rang out in her head.

Christelle's chest tightened and she pushed down the crazy urge to cry. She hadn't seen her mother since she was four! Staring at the woman, she couldn't mesh her heart's image with her mind's.

Whatever.

She pulled her arms around her knees. She *really* needed to work on her mind's privacy settings.

A faint brown glow in the distance distracted her from herself. Their coral platforms seemed to be headed directly for it, and it grew way faster than she'd expected.

How fast were they moving?

The glow deepened as the hint of ground rushed at them.

Ground!

She didn't mean to shout, or mind-shout, but the others jumped. Except Isamea.

And the ground solidified as they plummeted toward it. She had to do something!

But just before she swept in with some crazy, jacked up gift, the ground seemed to open up, a darkness spiraling below them. Their coral platforms somehow leveled out, without even a jostle in her bubble, and they sunk into darkness.

How…what…? Pekoi?

Pekoi, visible only through his uliee, shook his head slowly at her, hands turned up. He didn't seem able to speak, and that was saying something.

They sunk deeper, passing the ground, then into it. Slowly, as her eyes adjusted to the space, faint glowing energy reached her perception. Water, walls, and other coral platforms glowed in a space that resembled a marina. A really large, underwater marina. Was this Ys? If it was, how many Ysians lived here to need this big of a marina?

The Ysians swam off their platforms and suddenly she and Pekoi, still in their bubbles, were floating after the group, toward the far wall of the cavernous marina. As the group floated up, the wall swirled open and this time she was able to pay attention to how the openings worked. Isamea touched the wall and the brown energy within it spiraled, shifting the rock into an opening. And just like entering the volcanic caves back in Hawaii, they stepped into a large rock corridor filled with air, their bubbles popping as she and Pekoi stumbled onto the ground and into gravity, tumbling and rolling to a stop.

"Ugh." She lay next to Pekoi, assessing her body.

A few Ysians, standing by the wall they'd just entered through, approached Isamea and…saluted?

She noticed then that, although the Ysians seemed to be of many different ethnicities, they all had the same pale, color-shocked-out-of-it, white hair and they all wore a similar shirt and pants, grey with tiny gold threading, but no other colors. It all seemed so militaristic, not like any of the other Waker Communities.

She and Pekoi exchanged a look.

This is kind of creepy.

This time she hoped her settings were on ultra privacy. He nodded, and no one else seemed to notice.

"Report." Isamea demanded of the two.

"Commander, there's reports coming in about an attack in the Kao community. We've sent some scouts but they won't be back until tomorrow."

"Come directly to me when they're back, Captain."

The Captain nodded and lead the other Ysian down a tunnel to the right. Isamea turned abruptly and started down the large main tunnel, the others from the platform pushing Christelle and Pekoi hurriedly after her.

Christelle shook them off her, glaring. "Step back." When they didn't, she shoved them back with a bit of air. Actually, a wall of air that swirled between them and her, Pekoi next to her.

"Christelle." Isamea's tone was nothing but commanding.

She didn't even look back at her mother. "I don't like to be handled."

After a long moment, in which both sides glared but didn't move, Isamea sighed. "Dismissed."

The two Ysians' eyes morphed from slits to wide.

"Now." Isamea's tone left not even a thin crack for doubt.

They both nodded, threw a departing glare toward Christelle, then turned to head back toward the marina.

What was wrong with her mother? Or maybe Isamea had always been like this and Ys had always been a military place, full of hardened fighters. After all, back in Manatee Isles the first Ysian she'd met, Adrien, had arrived to teach everyone to fight. But her memories, the ones she'd gotten back, just didn't show her mother that way. Christelle needed time to figure this out, to hopefully rediscover the mother from those memories in the woman called Isamea.

She started after Isamea, Pekoi following, heading toward who knows where?

Somewhere up ahead, Christelle heard shouting and clanging. The stone walls muffled the loudness, but it seemed off to her left. As they moved, multiple voices settled out.

"Too weak!"

"I'm not."

A couple of thumps then a muffled whimper.

Without thinking, she ran towards the sound, stumbling to a stop at the mouth of a enormous cavern spilling off the corridor.

A child, no more than ten or twelve, lay curled up, a group of older children loosely ringed around her. An adult stood off to the side, apparently uninterested in doing anything but cross his arms while a boy, tall and broad shouldered, loomed over the girl. And kicked her.

Christelle's instinct kicked in again. She strode over to the group and stepped in front of the boy, Pekoi backing her up. "Back off." Christelle growled.

Suddenly, the adult's dulled expression focused on the group and he strode next to the boy. "This isn't your business."

Were all Ysians jerks? She hoped not, but so far things weren't looking great.

"Kicking kids should be *your* business, but you don't seem capable of dealing." Christelle's fists clenched.

He stepped right up to her, his stale breath hitting her face. Pekoi shifted, but she waved him back, then coughed out the scent of the man's breath.

"We don't abide weakness, or," the Ysian leaned in, his nose touching hers, "interference."

Then, with a blast of air, he was up against the ceiling. Surprise held him unmoving for a moment, then his uliee, strangely weak, whipped around him with no effect. That's when he froze a second time, but maybe in fear more than surprise.

Christelle glanced from the struggling ceiling ornament to the kids, the whole circle of students backing up, moving further away from her. And she had a brief glimpse of what Eka must feel like.

I wish you were here, Eka.

That was only for her mind.

"Christelle, enough." Isamea's voice was behind her, commanding again.

She looked up at the man, glaring. "Back off the kicking-little-kids-support and I'll let you down."

His eyes flicked to Isamea, then he nodded. Christelle sighed, guessing he was just doing what her mother wanted, and dropped him. The sound of his thud had nothing to do with her smile. Really.

Good job. Pekoi's voice somehow grinned inside her head.

Christelle turned and helped the little girl up. "You okay?"

The girl, freckles on pale skin bouncing with her nod, stared, mouth agape.

"Everyone, that's enough for today." Isamea stated, then turned toward Christelle. "You, with me."

Christelle huffed. "Fine." Then she kneeled down next to the girl. "What's your name?"

"Tanu."

"Do you need help going somewhere?"

Tanu crossed her arms and frowned. "I can take care of myself."

Christelle nodded, smiling. "I bet you can. But, if you ever need back up, come get me. Okay?"

Tanu nodded, a little smile on her face before she headed toward the far side of the space.

Isamea shook her head at the scene, scowling ever so briefly, then strode out.

"Guess we keep following?" Pekoi asked Christelle.

"Seems so." She and Pekoi straggled after Isamea for a turn of the corridor then halted behind a stopped Isamea.

"Mom?"

Isamea abruptly spun on Christelle. "We need to talk." Then, just as abruptly, she opened a door, into a room. Christelle stepped in, but Isamea stopped Pekoi. "I need to speak with her alone."

"Christelle?" Pekoi hung at the doorframe, waiting.

Christelle glanced at Isamea, then nodded. "It'll be fine. Be out soon."

His nod was cut off by the closing door.

"What is going on?" Christelle glared at her mother. But left out 'Who are you?'. The question she really wanted to ask.

Isamae stared at her, hands clasped behind her back. "Christelle." Her voice was so rigid, so controlled. "I know this must all be…different then what you're used to."

"Not really used to anything, actually." Christelle snipped, arms folding across her chest.

Pain, tiny and fleeting, passed across her mother's face. At least Christelle thought she saw pain. Maybe her mother was still in there.

"I never wanted to leave you, never wanted *them* to take away who you were. And I'm sorry for that." Isamae's hands tapped behind her back, energy roiling around. Then she stepped up to Christelle and laid her hand on Christelle's cheek. Christelle's breath caught as the woman seemed to soften before her and in that moment, a dozen memories of love and laughter all swirled around images of her mother. But before Christelle could seize this moment, to try to talk to the mother she faintly remembered, Isamea stilled. Hardened. Stepped back. "But it will never happen again." She still stared at Christelle, but as a commander, not her mother. "I will stop that thing. But I can't do that if we aren't strong."

"Abuse doesn't make anyone stronger."

Isamea stared for a long moment. "I spent a long time among the Asleep, hiding, waiting for any sign of that thing. And, while Asleep may be useless for most things," a snarl flitted across her features, "they have a great ability to train for effective destruction. To win."

Had her mother joined the special forces?

"The other Wakers are training with Ysians. Finally getting ready."

A laugh escaped Isamea. A tight, irritated, you-have-no-idea-what-you-just-said type of laugh. "Wakers are almost as weak as Asleep. They'd rather hide then deal with what's right in front of them."

Christelle flinched at the hint of truth in the broad statement. She would have grown up with parents if fear hadn't lead so many Wakers to hide from the truth. But not everyone.

"That monster is too strong for weakness." Isamea's body tensed more. "You have to understand, too many have died. If we go up against this thing unready we will all die. I've seen what it does."

"So have I." Christelle shuddered as sensations of shadow and cold and tearing slid through her.

Isamea's eyebrows raised. "Then you know. The attacks are increasing. Something is happening soon, and our community won't be ready unless we work harder."

Christelle thought about all the Wakers in Hawaii, gathered from so many other communities. They weren't trained, but they could be, and Ysians were trying to fix that. But, she knew training wasn't really much, not without a truly devastating weapon with a proper power source. Her own almost endless source of energy and Eka's ability to shield them could only help so much.

"Sema and Win did figure out a weapon that could stop Lintu. We're trying to spread it among the Communities and I promised to make sure everyone has a power source to run it."

Isamea nodded and…smiled. "I've heard about this weapon, it's exactly the break we needed. You can help us build one, learn how to use it."

Wait, did her mother just *smile*. Christelle could be part of preparing Ysians, a group that obviously wouldn't hero worship her. But, Yang and Eiriol were out there, helping other Wakers learn to make these devices, and she couldn't forget her part in that team. "I really need to help a huge number of Wakers, so they're ready to power up the weapons. I kinda promised."

Isamea waved away her words. "We can let all the communities know what to do."

"Um, I really have to do it in person. It's not about telling them how work the power on the device, I have to upgrade their energy." Christelle cringe-smiled.

"Upgrade?"

Now Christelle started pacing. So much had happened, but she really didn't want to sit down to hours, or maybe, days worth of explanation.

"Christelle!" Weak but pulsing uliee swirled around Isamea again.

Christelle frowned, her mother really needed to relax. Okay, just the highlights. "After I fought Lintu back in Manatee Isles, Gaia healed me, created a source inside me, and now I'm kind of a smaller version of her. At least energy wise." Isamea's brow furrowed at first, as if she were taking everything in, then raised in some crazy, facial gymnastics. "To power up the weapon, I have to upgrade other Wakers' energy. I can't make them a source, like me, but they're way stronger conduits for Gaia's energy."

Okay, that wasn't so hard.

Isamea was still staring at her, but now it was a squinting look, as if Christelle was a bug under a magnifying glass.

"I knew you looked a bit different from other Wakers, but you're Ysian, so of course you would." Isamea stepped right in front of her. "But I didn't realize just how incredible your energy had become. Christelle, you are exactly what we need!"

"But, I have to go to the other communities. I'll come back after, but I promised." She really wished she didn't but she couldn't put off that promise forever.

Another wave off. "You can upgrade Ysians and they can help the other communities, and ours."

That could work. Ysians were supposedly strong already so she could probably boast them easily. Although the ones she'd seen here seemed no stronger than any Wakers, maybe even weaker. Hopefully they weren't all like that.

Christelle looked at Isamea, the small glimpse of a mother, her mother, had been there. She just needed time to reach her. And, being part of her community, the one she was supposed to have grown up in, could be a great way to do that.

Christelle nodded.

"Wonderful!"

Just then the door burst open and Christelle's father flew past Pekoi and into the room. "Christelle!"

"Dad?" She blinked at the figure rushing towards her.

He swept her up in a hug and the moment they touched, tears flooded her eyes. She buried her head in his chest. "I missed you, Squirrel."

She used to hate his nickname for her, she wasn't just the sum of her aerial abilities. But now that she knew how much more she really was, she wished she was still just his squirrel. For a moment, at least. She squeezed him tighter until he huffed, a bit of a laugh underneath, and looked up at him, his hands brushing her tears.

"You look so…" He inhaled deeply. "Waker."

She nodded. "And you look tired."

His laugh rang through the room, a laugh she'd rarely heard from him, a soul laugh.

"We'll talk later." And just like that Isamea left the room, leaving her and her dad behind and completely avoiding the family reunion.

Eka Needs A Schedule

Starlight and energy mutely lit up the Austrian countryside and Eka took in all the colors and shadows as she swung her legs, sitting at the edge of the hayloft. Bits of old hay wafted around on a tiny breeze that was making its way out of the loft. She grabbed at the hay while swatting at the little air spirits. "Hey! That's my bed!"

The old barn shifted slightly as she continued to futilely grab at hay and she froze. Maybe the spirits were hinting at something by moving her bed a piece at a time.

"Like maybe this isn't the safest place to stay." Eka mumbled to herself.

She couldn't read the faded German signs around the property, but the barn seemed abandoned, and there was a town nearby with libraries. She hoped. Besides, not a lot of options with no credit card, bank account, phone, car.

Yep, this was it.

She patted the wooden planks which creaked just like her truck used to. "Hang in there a bit longer."

Creak.

Short answer but she'd take it as a positive.

This way of life was getting pretty tricky. Two toes in the Waker world, a pinky toe in the Asleep world, and a crazy shadow monster from another universe, that had killed her family, trying to get her to join it. And magic that was fun, but not so useful for tracking down information or getting her a place to stay.

"Glad I found my way back to this life." She sighed. "Yeah. So much better."

Uncovering this world and her past had done one thing for her, fear no longer was in charge. She wasn't running any more. Okay, she was running, but no longer from things, but to something and it was her choice, not a knee-jerk reaction.

"But would be nice to have some resources. A phone, maybe." Then she wouldn't have to go into town and hope English was in some kind of use here. She didn't even know what country she was in.

Suddenly, Mele streaked into the loft, chased by Fluffy. They shot around the barn, Mele dogging the wind as Fluffy swirled up and swatted at her.

Eka felt the barn sag another inch. "Hey! This place is holding on by a thread." Mele and Fluffy dove down next to her, the breezy cat looking up at her while Mele's rainbow form fluttering gently on the cat's head. She grinned. A wind-cat spirit and an energy bird as playmates. It really had been a long, strange journey.

"So Fluffy, didn't follow Pekoi, huh?" The cat-wind seemed to deflate and curl up, the breeze dying down to nothing. Mele sprang to Eka's face and fluttered, a definite chiding coming through.

"Oh, sorry." Did it miss Pekoi? She tried petting Fluffy, but her hand just went through.

Before the weird awkward moment drug out, a flash of familiar deep-space light streaked towards her and slammed into her. Eka and the light tumbled until a wall quick-stopped her, legs splayed up across it, face plastered to the floor as the barn dangerously swayed.

"Liney." She mumbled. "Great to see you."

Eka! I've been searching for you! You are not on the air ship. Glowing light coalesced into the familiar strawberry blonde and freckles.

Eka peeled herself off the wood and carefully crawled to a sitting position, back at the edge of the loft where Liney joined her. "I left the ship yesterday." A few pieces of hay, and other stuff she tried not to look at too hard, fell out of her short hair.

Mele and Fluffy, they came for me. Liney grinned then squinted at Eka's legs already swinging again. Liney started swinging her own legs too, mimicing Eka. *This is fun!* She swung faster and harder, throwing her body back and forth until she threw herself off the loft and into the air, righting the barn.

"Liney!" Eka instinctively yelled, but before she reacted, she remembered who was falling, as Liney dissipated into energy then coalesced again, sitting next to Eka. Eka just stared for a moment before looking at her own hands, legs, body. Had Eka really done that same thing, just a few days ago? How had she done it? Could she do it again? It definitely could be a useful skill.

Eka. Liney snapped her out of her thoughts. *Why are you here? Where are your friends?*

Eka sighed, like for the hundredth time tonight. "Christelle had to go somewhere and some of the others on the ship were…uncomfortable with me around."

Liney grasped Eka's hand. *I am sorry. I will comfort, with you.*

Eka smiled. "Thanks. Glad you're here." She squeezed Liney's had back, their deep space energy mixing. A tingling swept over her and then her arm faded at the wrist, her hand dissolving into uliee.

What the…

She'd gone energy.

Her brain lurched and the hand reappeared.

Eka? Liney frowned.

"I don't…it's so weird."

For this body to leave? Liney's hand reappeared as well.

Eka nodded. "My body just disappearing. It's weird." She took a deep breath. The sensation had startled her, but she didn't really feel like she wasn't there. But the visuals of no hand were really freaky. "It was kinda cool. Just weird."

Liney's head cocked to the side and she tapped Eka's shoulder. *This is part of you, this energy. It's bad to not accept you.*

"Okay, wise one, that's great for you. But it's all new for me." But, she was done running in fear. This was a part of her now and she needed to embrace her new life, outcast, strange magic, and all.

Strange magic. A reminder of the lighter's energy, a flash of deep space glowing within his Gaia energy, spun through her mind.

"Liney, have you ever met a Waker with energy like you, us?"

Liney frowned then shook her head. *No. But I stay away from them, so I do not look.*

Huh.

Maybe she was wrong. "It's just, I thought I saw a flash of energy, like mine, or yours, in one of the lighters."

Lighters?

"Yeah, the Wakers that can work with light, communicate with it, feed it."

Liney's eyes grew. *Oh!* She squirmed a bit in her seat. *But most light isn't from here, from Gaia. The energy for light, to feed it, is different. Maybe there is something in them from an else place.*

A twinge of something ran through her. Was it hope? Eka's spirits had suddenly lifted, so it seemed like it. But why would that make her hopeful? If what she saw was true, then that lighter didn't know he had a different kind of energy that could be non-Gaian. Or didn't want to know. He definitely didn't want anything to do with Eka. She wasn't a lighter, per se, so she wasn't carrying around the same energy as them, still…maybe she really did have a connection to the Waker world after all.

Yeah, right.

She shook her head. Lighters weren't exactly the norm for Wakers, even if they were valuable to Wakers community. And thinking these fringe Wakers could be like her in any way was a long shot. Besides, she had more things to do besides obsess over being an outsider. Lintu wasn't going to stop himself and she had one task to focus on, to find a weakness before he found her and caught her up in whatever destructive plans he had.

And then there was Ke. She still believed he might be out there and she could stumble onto a clue of what happened to him. But this was another long shot and unfortunately, long shots seemed to be piling up in her life these days.

Always best to just plow ahead with what's most manageable. Eka plastered a smile on her face. "Want to go look for where Lintu came from?"

What? Liney started to fade, but Eka grabbed her shoulder.

Wait.

Eka held her breath as Liney solidified again, but the energy coiled around her, ready to spring away. Eka deflated as her breath escaped. "Listen. Lintu is trying to find me, and I really don't know where to hide. And maybe, I don't want to hide forever." Liney seemed to relax a tiny bit and Eka dropped her hand. "But I don't know how to stop it. The Wakers have a device that seems to hurt him, and they're trying to make it better, hoping it can eventually destroy him. But, until then, I need to understand him so I can protect myself before he finds a way to use me for whatever he's doing."

They sat for a few moments staring at each other. Would Liney help? Eka wasn't sure where the next moment would take her, with a partner or alone again.

Liney slowly nodded and Eka's tension seeped away.

"Yeah!" Eka hugged Liney, then awkwardly released her to a brief smile on Liney's face.

I can't fight him, this Lintu. I don't know how I can help you, but I will try. Liney's smile faded a bit.

"You were there, came through with Irida and Lintu. Do you remember anything at all about the tear that you came through? How it was different than a portal? Any clue at all about where you where?" Eka crossed her fingers for a break. "Or the Waker you saw there, the woman who ran away?"

Liney shook her head. *The tear was cutting, like glass, nothing like a portal. It hurt. And when I fell through, this world, universe, it is so different than mine. I was also too confused, hurting, scared when I came through. Everything so jumbled. I just hid. Only until I found her, Irida, did I have hope of going home. Now she's gone.*

"You still believe you can get home, right?" Eka blurted out.

This time Liney sighed. *I don't know. But I will still try, I don't want to live alone forever. And that is how I am, here.*

Eka nodded. "I know." And she did. "How about this, do you think you would recognize the place if we found it?"

Maybe. We could try.

"Okay, then our mission, if we choose to accept it, is to find out where you came through, how it happened, stop Lintu, and get you home."

Really? Liney's ghost of a smile was all the commitment Eka needed.

"Yep. Ready to check out some old natural disasters?"

Two in the morning was always a bit magical, and eerie. A few scattered, white wooden buildings, made up the whole downtown and the closest train station was over the mountains. Luckily, when they'd scoured the library earlier, there'd been a train brochure, with a schedule and a map, otherwise, they'd of been s.o.l. Eka wished she knew the area better then they could just fly where they needed to go. But three different countries was a bit too large an area to hover around looking for a place Liney may or may not remember. And they hadn't even been able to narrow down the countries to Europe. They'd talked about portaling but even if she knew where they needed to go, would an image be enough information to portal there?

Probably not. She might end up in some wall or something weird, she'd seen it happen in movies.

So now, they were off to probable locations in the closest countries. How hard could it…nevermind.

Early morning hadn't come quickly enough. she was so antsy, hiding out in that barn, so ready to do something.

"Computers are very…uncomfortable." Liney rubbed her eyes.

Eka shook her head and rubbed ink off her hands. "Those weren't computers. They're newspapers." Who knew you needed id to check stuff out of a library.

Probably people who actually use libraries.

And luckily Liney was fluent in German. Kind of.

"So." Eka glanced at her. "When you flow through people, you can learn everything they know?" The world was getting weirder, and more interesting, every day.

I can understand and learn the strongest part of them. Language is in every part of humans." Liney cocked her head. *"Their voices, motions, hunger. Everything. The woman in the library, she was very hungry.*

Huh. Weird.

You can also move through others. When you aren't solid. Liney said this as if it were as common as walking down the road, not fantastical. How could floating through a person as an energy being, then absorbing a copy of their memories, not be fantastical?

Did she really want to try that? Becoming just uliee was really cool, but moving through another person? Maybe not. "Yeah. Anyway." Eka looked around the sleeping town. "Wish we could portal." Liney nodded in agreement.

Eka thought Liney, having traveled the planet over the years, would be able to portal them to places she'd been. But Liney didn't know the names of the places, except from the memories of the few people who she'd flowed through and none of those people had traveled much. And Eka wasn't sure how to explain where they needed to go as she hadn't been to any of the places on their list, leaving descriptions, images and videos from the library. On top of it all, Liney had said that they needed the 'feel' of a place to portal, whatever that was.

Unfortunately they had a lot of ground to cover to travel by 'normal' means. They'd tried to stick to Europe and the story they'd heard, but there were a lot of disasters that had happened around the world during the major world wars, which is the time period they were starting with. The most encompassing wars that included the most countries. After that, they'd have to look at more and more local wars. This really was a needle in a haystack situation and they needed some major luck.

Liney just nodded. She didn't seem to know the scope of their self-appointed task.

"Okay, so no car. We're flying to…Mt. Marmolada in Italy. An avalanched area in 1916 is probably not the place, but it's close." Eka winked and pulled out her marble. "Ready?"

Yes. Liney nodded. *But I think it's easier to become less solid.* And with that thought, Liney dissipated into a shimmer of deep space energy and floated above the dark town.

Oh Yeah.

Eka took a calming deep breath.

Okay. I've done this. Hope I can read the map while I'm haze. And hope I can hold it.

She let go of herself and her breath, feeling the moonlight, starlight, and all the energy around her call to her, mixing in with her. Then, she was floating, pieces held together by her mind, her spirit, hovering next to Liney.

Woot woot!

Yeah! Liney answered back.

And then they were headed over the mountains, under the bright night sky, a solitary map floating away in the wind.

Christelle Needs Some Air

The trainer, with his military garb and cutting gaze, almost demanded his words be obeyed as he barked out instructions. "Let the air sink into your skin. Deep your body warm. Keep the pressure pushing out."

Uh, yeah.

Then the water swirled overhead as another pair of feet disappeared up into the hole in the ceiling, harsh lighting outlining the ripples left by those feet. Christelle blinked, sweat dripping down her nose and cheeks. What was she thinking? She'd only been here a day, she wasn't ready to try breathing underwater.

I'm not a fish!

Pekoi stood in front of her and Jake squeezed her arm. She hadn't realized how glad she was they both were here.

"Hey, you don't have to do this." Pekoi stared straight at her. "No one needs you to."

Except my mom.

"It's not really hard." A small voice whispered next to her. Christelle looked down to find Tanu wearing the strangely suit all the swimmers had on, including her. It was almost like a skin tight yoga top and shorts, but in those stupid, dull military colors everyone wore here. She could feel air passing through it, though, and guessed she'd need all the air she could get next to her skin. At least there was one cool thing about this outfit.

"Really?" Christelle squeaked unexpectedly at Tanu.

Wearing the determination of a runner facing a marathon, Tanu nodded, so serious for someone so young. Then she motioned Christelle down to her level, which wasn't that far.

Christelle bent over and Tanu whispered just for her. "It's not so bad. It kind of tickles."

Christelle stood and took a deep breath.

If this small girl can jump into water and breath, then she could get it together and do the same. Besides, what would Eka think?

Woot woot!

Christelle grinned briefly, nodding. "I think I can handle that."

Tanu motioned toward the water without even cracking a tiny smile, then a swift swirl of air lifted her small form up and her head, then body, was swallowed by the reflective opening in the ceiling.

Their trainer, wearing an expression matching the dull and empty uniform of Ys, nodded Christelle over. Around his neck, he also wore a strangely smokey crystal as he stood ready to help her into the depths of the ocean.

What was it with those crystals so many of the Ysians wore?

Before she could form the question for him, weak wind, called by the trainer, lifted her up into wet, freezing, crushing liquid. Christelle's brain stopped, as a frozen vice-grip squeezed her body into itself. She couldn't open her eyes enough to remember to focus on getting back to the tunnel.

Die! I'm going to die!

Panic-brain swept over her as she floated in an freezing hellscape.

A tiny pinpoint of warmth grabbed her attention, spreading across her hand, then around her whole body. Christelle blinked until Tanu's small, blurred body floated in front of her, a little hand in Christelle's as Tanu's blanket of warmth and protection covered them both.

It's kind of cold at first. Tanu's small voice floated through her head.

Christelle nodded shakily.

But, before she could even enjoy the warmth, another problem gripped her. Air. Too little of the oxygen stuff and lungs tend to take notice. And hers were on high alert.

Through my skin! I don't know what that means! Stupid, stupid, stupid!

She flailed, reaching for the tunnel, but the warm, little hand held on. More tightly than Tanu seemed capable of.

Try. The small voice encouraged and a feeling swept over her, of tingling and tickling running up and down her skin. Of air, or maybe just parts of it, passing through her from the water around her. Her skin, and body, were breathing in water! How, why, she had no clue, but she was breathing!

She finally opened her eyes and…she could see clearly! This was so weird, seeing in dark water as if she was up on land. Had her vision changed? Permanently? She hadn't even felt a change. Had she always been able to do this? All around her, bits of energy dimly glowed. A bit more dimly than she was used to, but maybe there was less life here.

It was like the little bit of encouragement had jumped started these gifts.

You want to swim? Tanu's voice whispered inside her, the little hand no longer holding hers, but Christelle was still warm. Just ahead, the child wiggled, like a mermaid, in figure eights.

Okay. I'm breathing through my skin, keeping my body warm in freezing temperatures, and can see clearly underwater. Why not?

And, with a wiggle of her legs, she shot around in a loop, then barrel rolled to the opening, skimming her fingers along the barrier.

I'm a freakin' mermaid!

A what? Tanu asked.

Christelle giggled and shared an image with the girl.

Weird. Tanu obviously didn't get the cool factor.

Christelle shook her head, giggles dying. Some things were just beyond Wakers. Before she could explore her surroundings further, the other Ysian trainees arrived back from their swim training and dropped into the tunnel. Tanu motioned for her as the girl dropped out of the ocean too. Christelle reluctantly headed back, taking one last loop then dove into the cave.

And hit the air. Her body dropped straight through the air and onto the floor, rolling a few feet.

"Oghff." She sprawled face down on the rock.

"Christelle!" Pekoi and Jake ran to her side, flipping her over as her lungs kicked back into gear.

Fuzzy forms slowly focused for her as she blinked. "That…was…great!" She wheezed.

"You're okay!" Jake beamed down at her. "You did amazing!"

Pekoi grabbed her hand and gently pulled her up, grinning. "The landing was a bit off, though."

"You…try…next…time." She narrowed her eyes, a grin fighting for air.

"Your Ysian side is returning. Very good." Christelle turned around to find Isamea, her command uniform without a wrinkle, standing with arms crossed.

"My Ysian side." Christelle whispered, feeling her body finish shifting gears to breath fully with her lungs.

Isamea nodded and strode over then grasped Christelle's shoulders. "I never had the chance to show you how to swim, truly swim, like we do." Isamea's eyes glassed over. Was her mother about to cry? "I'm so glad you're home."

Her own eyes were definitely watering. Her mom was glad she was here. Glad! Christelle's hand clamped over her mother's. "Me too."

"Um." One of the swimming trainers coughed and Isamea blinked, dropping Christelle's hand. "The trainees are ready for sparing."

Damnit.

Christelle glanced at the moment-destroying trainer, glaring.

"Go ahead and start them, I'll be there soon." The woman nodded at Isamae and led the three other swimmers down a side tunnel. Tanu stayed, dwarfed by Pekoi and Jake.

"Christelle." Isamea turned back toward Christelle. "I need you to do something for me."

"Really?" Her mother needed her? She could definitely use time with Isamea.

"Our technicians need more help to understand the weapon you used in Hawaii. Your description wasn't enough to start building one so they would appreciate your assistance."

"Oh." Helping assistants. Great. "I really don't know much more than I told them, but I could try."

Isamea seemed to see through her, know what would work on her. "Anything you know would be a great help. To me."

Christelle took a deep breath and nodded.

"Wonderful." Isamea nodded back. "Tanu can show you the lab." She turned to leave, heading toward the hall the others had disappeared down. As Isamea passed Jake, he tried to speak to her, but she didn't even glance at him.

Was she mad at him? "Dad?"

Jake coughed and turned from Isamea's disappearing form. "Better get to that lab. I'll catch up with you later." And he bolted down a lonely little tunnel that no one else seemed to be using.

What was happening? They were finally all together. No more hiding, pretending, lying. This should be *the* reunion.

Stop. Every family had down times. Training seems to be mom's thing. Get the device working for them and I can work with mom to train others. We'll have some time together. And maybe dad could join us then too.

"Um." Pekoi grimaced. "I seem to ask this a lot, but, you okay?"

"Yeah. Maybe." She shrugged then took a very long breath. "I guess we're going to the lab. Tanu?"

Tanu, who had remained so silent, just nodded ever so briefly, then started down yet another tunnel. As they walked along, the stark lighting here, like everywhere else, almost drowned out any energy glow from the wall and if she wasn't entered the water through the ceiling of an underground cavern, Christelle could believe she was back in the Asleep world.

"How many tunnels are there?" Pekoi asked quietly.

"Way too many." Christelle answered in her own quiet voice, not sure why. "I can't remember how I got here. Glad we have a guide." Christelle tried to smile, but she just wasn't feeling light-hearted.

Pekoi took her hand and she noticed even *his* grin was missing.

Welcome frickin' home.

Eka Finds A Stone

Wind whipped around the small shield Eka'd created around her and Liney, atop the train headed for Villa San Giovani. They were headed to Messina, over the bay from Villa San Giovani and the epicenter of a devastating earthquake and tsunami. Technically, the events happened a few years before WWI, not during it, but it was one of the closest events to Austria on their list, so they might as well check it off first.

Since they were traveling during the day, as well as night, Eka had managed to bend light around them, holding both invisibility and the shield in place without any issues. She wasn't even sure how she did it, blending the different energies within her to work this magic. But somehow it did work, sparking a bit of excitement and maybe even pride in Eka.

"My magic is actually kicking ass." A grin spread across her face and a giddiness spread across her whole body.

As the train sped over the countryside and through towns, she caught bits of energy sparkling within the Italian landscape, more muted than the Waker communities, but still flowing through the life around her, which now included her. Her uliee entwined with the purely Gaian energy as trees and ocean flew by and wind caught her short hair, dancing around the strands and tickling her cheeks.

When had she become so connected to everything? Not exactly the way Wakers connected, she couldn't get the wind to lift her up, or water droplets to form out of dew, that would be crazy. But somehow, all the spirits around her were comfortable with her now, like she was one of them.

Eka stretched her legs, the ache of sitting in the tiny room she'd made for them on the back of the train, slowly disappearing, and she lay back. If only there weren't any tunnels, she'd have slept on the roof.

Of course, portaling would have been easier, but Liney's warning flitted through her mind again, reflecting her own thoughts. 'When you haven't been already, have a feeling of a place, you might get stuck in stone. Or a building. That is not fun.'

The image of a leg sticking out of an old Italian building danced through her mind. Nope, that wouldn't be fun at all. But would she really have messed up?

"Blah, blah, blah. I could've done it."

Little bits of rainbow energy abruptly flowed around her and coalesced into Mele, chattering from his perch on her crossed hands.

"I don't know when we'll be there."

A tiny breeze ruffled Mele's feathers and the bird looked around.

Was Mele nervous?

It squeaked and Eka shook her head and shrugged.

"I haven't seen Fluffy…" But her voice died as a gust bounced across her legs and slammed into Mele. Eka blinked as Fluffy and the bird tumbled down the back of the train.

Fluffy was getting way stealthier, Eka grinned and crawled to the edge. The two little spirits were gone but the ground was slowing and buildings started crowding the tracks, which meant their station was ahead. This was their first destination, could they be lucky enough to hit gold on the first go?

"Why not? Someone eventually wins the lottery." Eka mumbled and went to find Liney.

Eka leaned on a column in the station, holding a brochure. Obviously not reading it, she'd never learned any other language but English, but she was doing her best to look like Italian was her native tongue. Of course, Liney pulled her float-through-people-to-learn-what-they-know trick and soon *was* reading like a native.

Eka cocked her head, studying her friend. Liney made it look so easy, but she just wasn't ready to flow through someone else, experiencing their memories and their knowledge. Sure, that part might be cool, but what else did you experience?

She shuddered. She wasn't finding out today.

We have to cross some water. Liney walked past Eka, leading her out of the station to stare at the bay. *We need to go there.*

Across the bay to Messina, according to the map. Eka could faintly make out buildings on the other side. "Lead the way."

They chose a spot on the water, far from any prying eyes. No need for any Asleep to see two people dissolve into nothing and luckily they couldn't see any Gaian energy or uliee. Or extra-Gaian uliee, as was the case for this pair. She couldn't imagine what any Asleep would do if they could see them as Standing near the shore, stars lightly reflected off the still surface of the water, and Eka's body slowly relaxed and drifted apart. This was the weirdest part. And how could it not be weird, watching her foot dissolve into bits of light, energy, and flow out over a body of water. How did it not hurt? How did her mind stay in tact?

Who knows?

No one, apparently. Not even Liney, who seemed to exist naturally as bits floating around. To her, bodies were heavy and squishy.

Ahead, Liney's energy swirled and spiraled, Fluffy leaping through the spirals while Mele flitted around Eka as she drifted between landmasses and unanswered questions.

Three days later and Eka wasn't sure why she was on this quest. Nothing looked familiar to Liney and Eka had no other idea how to identify the area. What if Liney couldn't recognize the place anymore, how would they find it? The chances the Waker Liney had seen running away would still be in the area were slim to yeah, right. Besides, the only thing Liney remembered was that the woman was taller than Eka, paler than Eka, and had dark hair like Eka. Liney really hadn't spent much time around humans. But who could blame her for spending most of her time off-world, looking for others like her and avoiding Lintu.

And what was Eka hoping to find, if Liney did recognize the site? A magical recipe on how to destroy Lintu, just waiting for them in some old building, decades later? This was such a crapshoot, even for her.

"Ugh!"

Eka? Liney, dusty from walking through the hills around Messina, stopped trudging.

"Sorry, just tired."

And done with this whole thing.

But what else would she do? Going back to the Asleep world was out of the question, but there really weren't any Waker communities she could join. She really didn't have anywhere. Besides, Lintu would find her, sooner or later.

Eka. Liney, staring out over a cliff, toward an abandoned building, tapped her shoulder. *I feel something…familiar.*

"What?" Eka walked eagerly next to her, scanning the horizon. Then, a tiny, barely-there-unless-you-are-intently-trying-to-notice-it tickle skirted the edge of her awareness. "What is it?"

I…don't know. Liney whispered as she dissolved and flowed down the ragged cliffside towards the building below.

Eka followed, the tickle morphing to a tingle, then a whole body itch with a side of exhilarating anticipation. Something weird and wonderful was down there.

Liney skirted trees and rocks then swirled to her solidness and dropped to the ground, Eka coalescing next to her to just stare down at the ground. What was that feeling? It really did feel like her own energy, but there didn't seem to be anything there.

Liney gently touched the ground with her finger and, where her finger pressed, the hint of an energy tendril gently rose, wandering over her fingertip, sparking the uliee in her. Liney pulled her hand back, just staring at it.

Eka squatted down. "It's…"

My people's energy. Liney couldn't seem to pull her gaze from her hand. "But how?"

Liney shook her head.

Eka reached for the dirt. The same faint tendril rose up around her hand and then everything seemed to disappear. The echos of deep space surrounded her for a moment, then the faint impressions of portals zipped past her awareness, portals to other places. Places of extreme light, another of bubbles and lightness, a raging place of heat and burning. Then, a shiver ran over her. The sense of a cold, dead universe. Even though she wasn't there, she still couldn't seem to move, just float in the blankness of the place, like she couldn't even breath. Then, she jerked back and was in the dirt again, next to Liney whose hand was on her shoulder.

What was that?

Eka rubbed her cold, numb hand, then stared at it, probably like Liney was. But, how had her hand gone cold? Was she really there? It seemed more like a movie, but also one she was kind of in. And where were all those other places? That last one, though, she could never know where that one was and stay a happy person.

"Liney, I…that was traveling? Like your family?"

Liney looked at her, then at the ground. *I…don't know. Maybe…* Her face scrunched up, like she was trying to hold on to something. Hard. *…a story from my family. A story of travel, and doors, and passages…* Then her face dropped and she shook her head again, shoulders sagging. *I was so little, I don't remember.*

Travel and doors and passages. That was…surprisingly descriptive of her sensation when the strange and familiar energy had touched her. "No helpful answers. Sounds about right for magic." Eka scooted around in a circle, placing her hand on the ground around the strange spot. But it remained that, a strange spot, isolated and alone.

"Do you feel anything else?"

Liney shook her head, again. Eka sighed. There were way too many head shakes, when they needed a nod, followed by an explanation.

Eka finally took a look around the area. There was no town near this site, not even a farmhouse or ruins in the vicinity. Nothing indicating civilization or people and no sign of Wakers in the area, no uliee, just the natural energy coursing around her. How was this here without even a marker?

She turned to Liney. "Do you feel any Wakers or anyone near here?" Someone must know something about this.

Another head shake from her partner in cluelessness.

This is very old. Liney dug around in a small bag she carried. *Maybe before Wakers and Asleep were different.*

"Before their war?" Eka frowned as this just got trickier. Wakers may live a long time, but she was pretty sure none of them were tens of thousands of years old. "Wow." No wonder there wasn't anything left to mark it. Or anyone around to ask about it. Maybe when she met back up with Christelle, she would have more information on old legends, maybe a clue about why this energy was here.

"Alright." Eka stood. "I think we should move on, check out the other places on our list." What else could they do? They'd scoured the area of the earthquake, even gone back over to Villa San Giovani and checked for anything unusual, like this energy source, but found nothing until this moment.

Liney didn't answer. Instead, she held her hand over the spot, closed her eyes, and sang. The sound didn't reach Eka's ears, just her mind. Inside her, energy hopped and twirled toward Liney. Eka wrapped her arms around her body, focusing on holding herself in, while wisps of deep space energy rose from the ground and into a stone Liney now held in her hand.

Where'd that stone come from? Eka leaned towards it, glowing with the same deep color as Liney's uliee, but with flecks of gold scattered throughout it.

The last bit of energy from the strange spot disappeared into the stone and it dissolved into Liney's hand.

"What was *that*?"

Liney stood. *That's our memory holder for traveling. Helps us remember where we've been. And to share memories, so we can jump to new places easily.*

A sharable memory stone. With storage. Eka so needed one of those. "Maybe you have some memories there for our destinations?" It was a longshot but she had to ask.

But how would I know? Your names are empty, they feel like nowhere?

"Fair enough. Names really don't do much for me either." How many names had slipped in and out of her memory as they traveled? Too many to count.

Eka. Liney had that scrunched up look of concentration. *I feel my people in this energy. I don't know why this is here, but I can't leave it, so I store it.* She tapped the stone.

Ke's smile danced through her head and Eka nodded. "Yeah. I get it."

Maybe they both could find their families, or at least answers to where they might be and how to find them. "Should we try the next place on the list?"

Liney took a deep breath and slowly turned in a circle, then nodded. *Nothing else here.*

"Right."

Off in the distance, the train beckoned as they headed out. If they really had missed something, they could always come back. But Eka hoped they didn't.

Christelle Chases A Mouse

Christelle hung in the semi-dark water, a shadow sliding toward her out of the distance. She raised her hands.

Not yet.

Expanding at a rapid rate, the shadow took shape as a slit within it, rushing at her. She braced herself.

Not yet.

She tensed as the shadow, closer now, became a wide, pale wall, still speeding toward her. Then, inches from her, the wall came into focus and a whale slid next to her as she grabbed the corner of its mouth and hung along its side as it ploughed on. Abruptly, it shot upwards, cutting through the water as Christelle pulled in air from the water speeding by her until they finally broke the surface and the whale breeched, sending her tumbling down its side. Christelle instinctively balled up briefly then managed two forward spins and a layout, before diving back into the ocean. She hung under the gentle waves, the enormous whale sliding back next to her after a few barrel rolls under her. She patted its side, amazed at how rough the skin felt.

An image from the whale, of another go round, flitted through her mind and she shook her head.

Thanks but I'm beat, better head back.

She floated just long enough to catch the fin that slid by, and the whale dove toward Ys.

Eka would've loved this.

She dove the last half herself, eventually dropping into the opening of the cavern and padding over to her dry clothes.

"Hey sweetheart." Jake leaned against the side of a tunnel, fidgeting with his jean pockets. She knew that fidget, a nervous one.

"Dad?"

"So," he picked up a towel and handed it to her as they made their way to her workshop. "How's your project going?"

The Ysians had tried to build a device, but their attempt was so far off the mark, Christelle thought they were trying to build a machine gun out of natural materials lying around, which was weird, because no one in the Waker world used Asleep weapons, or needed to.

She had ended up taking over to try to recreate the device she'd 'plugged in to' back in the volcano. It had seemed, from that experience, that all the types of Gaian gifts needed to be represented in the contraption, so now her workbench sat covered in feathers, glass orbs filled with water, oil-soaked rags, tiny bellows, and dozens of other pieces. There had seemed to be an order to how each piece was activated when she'd used the one in Hawaii, an individual piece activated then, in turn, it activates the next piece, but she just couldn't figure out that order. At all. She'd spent a week configuring and reconfiguring these pieces into what she thought was a recreation of the device, but each attempt yielded nothing but smoke and flames and a soaked workbench. This whole puzzle was picking at her brain and her last nerve.

Her next biggest struggle was in figuring out what type of material to use for each Gaian gift in order to hold the largest energy charge. Oil seemed to hold a big charge and was easily burned, becoming the fire gift, but it could also spill on the other components and if fire burned up the entire device, then anyone using it would be left in a fight with no weapon. Flint, on the other hand, could represent earth and create fire, but it wasn't as great for storing energy. Besides, no matter what they used, fire could still burn up everything. Fire was pretty tricky. Then there was water. Try not soaking everything when adding water to a fighting device. She sighed at the memory of turning earth into mud and smothering the fire. How had any version of this thing stopped Lintu, back in Hawaii? And how was she supposed to improve it to hopefully kill him?

If only she had paid attention back in Hawaii when A'he tried explaining what Sema and Win had discovered to create the device, but she'd been worried about Eka, after losing Sema, and worried about Pekoi, not knowing he was okay. Besides, she thought her job was to upgrade the energy of the Wakers she met. Now she was stuck in Ys without a way to contact A'he, Ping, or Eiriol to ask how to make this thing. She'd even take Win, even though he was so shut down last time she'd seen him, she couldn't image he'd actually be much help.

So she'd effectively wasted her chance to understand how it worked and was stuck with just bits of her memory, from when she used the device and what she had read in that ancient Waker text. She really wished the Ysians had a copy of that book.

She scanned her workplace and sighed. This whole thing reminded her of that stupid game Mouse Trap.

A deadly mouse trap.

Ugh.

"Always hated that game." She mumbled as she dried off, shivering in the chilly cave.

"What game?" Jake leaned on his elbow, head in palm, staring at the pieces on the workbench.

"Mouse Trap." She sighed.

Jake glanced at her, hint of a smile on his face. "Is that why you cheated?"

"I didn't cheat." Christelle frowned.

Jake raised his eyebrows. "Oh, the board just managed to topple over every time I was winning?"

Christelle shrugged, trying not to grin. "The table always wobbled." And that's the story she was sticking to.

"Uh huh." He grinned at her. "You know, I really wish you could have met your grandparents."

"I know my grand…wait, mom's parents?" She had no memories of Isamea's parents so had excitedly asked about them when they first arrived in Ys. Unfortunately, her Mom had told her never to mention them again, then stormed out so quickly that Christelle had avoided the topic ever since that failed conversation. Her stomach clinched in anger as she was reminded, like a punch in the gut, of her lost childhood and lack of openness from those closest to her.

"They were pretty awesome, when I met them." He looked around the cave, obviously unaware of Christelle frustration and hurt. "And this place was so much more alive. So many Ysians. They really loved to perform, and laugh, and the colors. They'd dress up anything that wasn't moving, in crazy colors. And their gifts were so different, like they were not solid sometimes." He stared at a wall, as though there was a movie playing, or some memory recorded there. Then he chuckled. "I swear, I thought I saw one walk *through* a wall." He shook his head. "But, that was a long time ago."

Despite her anger, Christelle's curiosity kicked in. Jake had been so unavailable recently, almost shutting whenever she asked about his knowledge about this Community. Now he was almost giving her a personal history of Ys.

As she listened, she wondered how long ago was he talking about? No one here wore any colors except those weird military type outfits. And forget laughing, she wasn't sure they knew how. And special gifts? She hadn't notice any real gifts being used here and definitely hadn't had any luck upgrading any of the Ysians. It was like they had energy constipation or something. Come to think of it, that Ysian in Nova Scotia hadn't been upgradable either. Were the Ysians broken? Just another mystery she couldn't solve, but she could find out about her Ysian family and how this place changed.

"What happened here? And where are my grandparents now?" And so many more questions.

Jake's whole body tensed, a grimace overshadowing the wonder of the old memory. "I don't know. I asked Isamea, but she didn't answer. Just ignored it, like everything these days."

What was going on with her mom? "Dad, do you think…" Now Christelle played with the towel, not making eye contact. "Do you think she cares about us?"

Jake, without hesitating, strode to her side and grabbed her hands in his. Her head jerked up. "Isamea loves you very much. Don't ever doubt that." He sighed and stopped squeezing her hands so hard. "I don't know what happened to your mom, but she left everything to try to get your memories back, your life back."

Christelle nodded, still waiting for more.

"I guess she just needs time, maybe." Jake sighed, and Christelle wondered if he meant Isamea needed more time before she would be okay with her Dad. But he put on his 'I'm done talking about it' face and started playing with her fingers. Fidgeting again.

She wrapped the towel around her with her free hand and stilled her dad's fingers with her other hand. "Okay, you're fidgeting. What are you up to?"

"Never did learn to hide my hands." Jake shook his head. "Christelle, I've got to go to Hapton's for a bit."

"What? You're leaving? But, you just got here and I finally know about this world. We haven't had any time to talk about it all."

Jake swept her up in a hug. "You can't even imagine how happy I am you have your true self back. It almost killed me, what happened." After a moment, he set her down and stood back, looking her over. "And I want us to be a family again. But right now so much is going on with the attacks and your mother…" he stopped himself and shook his head, seeming to shake out thoughts of Isamea. "Anyway, I haven't heard from anyone in Hapton's, or anywhere else." He frowned and stared a moment at a wall and mumbled to himself. "It's so different here now." Then he shook his head again and refocused on Christelle. "I know you and Anise didn't leave on the best terms, but she's my sister and I need to know her and Mom and Dad are okay."

Christelle nodded again. She still hurt from losing her childhood, but after all the mess ups she'd done in Hawaii, where people almost died, she had little energy to judge her Aunt Anise anymore. "I get it. I'm worried about them too."

Jake flashed a quick smile. "You can come with if you want. It's gotten a bit weird around here."

Leave? Did she want to go? She had come here to get to know her mom, but Isamea had left right after they got here and been gone for nearly a week, still chasing Lintu. So why was she staying? Isamea may love Christelle, but did she even care to know her daughter again?

No, she has to care.

Christelle had seen that look when she'd first seen Isamea again, back in Ireland. Maybe it was brief, but it was there. And there were other moments where she saw the soft, loving mother from her returning memories.

There were also all the other times when Isamea was a hard woman Christelle didn't recognize at all. Maybe she should go for now and hope

Isamea, her loving mother, finally came back for good and found her.

Then Christelle remembered the device, her promise, the danger from Lintu, and the hope of ancient secrets the Ysians might have that could help destroy the danger they all faced. So far she hadn't discovered any lost weapons or old technologies, but legends were usually based on something and the Ysians were nothing if not legendary protectors of Gaia.

She shook her head and tried to smile. "Gotta finish this. But, promise you'll come back soon."

He cupped her cheek. "Promise." Then he kissed her forehead. "We'll be back before you know it."

"We?" Who else was going?

Jake grimaced. "Um, I wasn't supposed to be the messenger. You should check with Pekoi."

"Pekoi? He's leaving too?" What was happening?

Her hugged her again then headed out of the lab as she quickly changed. As she sprinted to her room, her heart pounded and she pushed back tears, finally sliding through the open doorway to find Pekoi packing the few things he had.

When she finally found him, he was packing his few things.

Pekoi looked up and smiled tightly. "Christelle, I…"

"You're leaving?" Had her heart just stopped?

"Um." Pekoi looked at his hands, then up at Christelle. "I, um, yeah."

"Why?" Was everyone lining up to leave?

Pekoi stood up from the bed and hesitantly stood in front of her, his eyes looking deep into her as his breath warmed her face.

"I get that you need to be here. Your mom, the device. Learning about your world here."

"It's not my world, just…" Christelle jumped in but Pekoi held up his hands.

"I love you, us. That hasn't changed. And I'm not leaving you." He leaned in, his eyes inches from hers. "I promise."

His eyes held her, like they always did, and his hands gripped hers now, sending his uliee into her, warming her and making other promises. She nodded.

After forever, he sighed. "I just need to do something…productive and that's not happening here. I feel I'd be more useful going with Jake to find out what's happening outside Ys."

Christelle realized she hadn't heard any news from outside Ys for the entire week she'd been here. She really tried not to dwell on how autocratic this place was beginning to feel, so different than the other Waker Communities she'd experienced. Maybe Jake and Pekoi could be more useful out there, not just to check on loved ones, but let others know what was going on here.

Still, her heart ached and he wasn't even gone yet.

"I won't be gone forever. Besides, we're going see your other community, Hapton. I bet Jake can tell me all your childhood secrets." He winked.

"Better not." She wiped her eyes and smiled.

"Hey." He smoothed her hair and leaned in, this time close to her ear. "You sure you don't want to come. Things here are a little…tense."

She inhaled deeply and shook her head. He was right, but she needed to finish this. If not for her mom, then for her community. "I'll be fine."

Pekoi looked her over before nodding. Then he leaned in and kissed her, soft, gentle and a little sad.

This time, swimming didn't shake her bad mood. Even introducing Tanu to Fin couldn't wipe out the cloud over her. When she finally climbed out of the water, she dug the towel into her hair and rubbed, probably giving herself scalp burn.

"Your head do something to you?" Tanu eyed her as the girl dried herself, a bit more gently than Christelle.

Christelle threw down the towel. "This whole, stupid life is what's wrong. I can't get any Ysians to upgrade, no one wants to talk about my grandparents, or anyone else that used to be here, and this place is so dull, I want to pull my hair out!" Why hadn't she left with Pekoi and her dad? How could a week alone seem so long?

"And, I can't even get that device to work better. It really is like mouse trap." She'd been joking before, but now, getting the pieces to fit and set one another off, was driving her nuts.

"Mouse trap?" Tanu frowned at her.

Christelle waved her off. "It's a game we played, Dad and I."

"You trapped mice for a game? Why?" Tanu, eyebrows raised, focused on Christelle.

"Not a real mouse." Christelle shook her head. "A fake mouse."

"Fake?" Tanu's brow furrowed deeper. "How do you have a fake mouse?"

"It'a a little plastic mouse that you move around a board." Christelle tried to gage the size of the plastic with her fingers. "About this big."

"Plastic?"

Christelle sighed. "It's an Asleep thing."

"Oh." Tanu huffed and crossed her arms.

"Hey." Christelle frowned. "What's wrong?"

"That's what everyone says when they don't want you to know something."

"I'm not hiding anything." Christelle hated the idea anyone would think that. "How about I show you?"

Tanu perked up. "Really?"

"Yep." Christelle nodded. "After I get that device working, I can take you up top and show you some Asleep stuff."

"Wow. My parents were going to take me before…" Tanu trailed off, looking at her hand.

What is it with everyone's parents? Before Tanu could protest, Christelle wrapped her in a hug. The girl tensed for a moment, then slowly hugged Christelle back. Maybe not a bear hug, but a good hug anyway.

"Okay." Christelle finally let go. "That was a great swim and I'm not going to let uptight Ysians and hard problems ruin the mood."

"About time." Tanu let a bit of a smile emerge. "Swimming with a whale is nice."

"Nice? How about incredible. How many times does a whale make surfing waves? Not many."

"Surfing was pretty nice."

Nice. Christelle shook her head. "Okay. Enough about mouse traps, surfing, and waves. I think…" Wait, waves. What if the device wasn't similar to that in-game mouse trap that activates each piece in turn, but more like, like a wave that gets bigger with each pebble added to the pond at the right time. "I think I've got it! Get dressed, we need to get back to the lab!"

"What are…" But Tanu's voice faded as she threw on her clothes, getting lost in her thoughts.

Tanu tried to keep up with Christelle as she barreled toward the lab.

"So you figured it out?" Tanu shouted as she sped after Christelle

"Maybe." Christelle glanced at Tanu. "But I need to check out some things."

Tanu's eyes grew larger and she reached out for Christelle just as she collided with another Ysian. Christelle stumbled as the stiff guy tumbled backward.

"Oh. Sorry." Christelle tripped a few more times then caught herself. She turned and walked toward the man, who was already standing, brushing off the familiar uniform. A small, dark blue shard lay at his feet. She picked it up, and murkiness slid briefly into her hand. "Yuck." She shook her palm at the itchy energy. "Is that energy?"

The Ysian yanked it from her and stormed off, without a word.

"What just happened?" Christelle frowned at the crazy guy's back.

Tanu shrugged. "Rude. Like all of them."

Again she was wondering why she hadn't left with Jake and Pekoi. "Let's just get back to the lab."

Eka Travels...A Lot

Eka stretched, enjoying the walk after riding so long on the outside of transportation, discorporated. She'd never been to Turkey, but hills and dirt really seemed to be a common landscape theme in their recent travels. And they needed to find another way to get places. Riding on the outside of planes was definitely not cool. It had sounded cool at first, and Eka pictured them with a little enclosure, just a shield protecting them, like on the train. But, crap it was cold. And holding a shield, staying invisible, and keeping warm, all at the same time for hours, was a bit too much, even for her new gifts. So they'd ridden in solid form inside the dark and cramped baggage area, only worried about heat, and only venturing out for brief moments.

No more planes. Liney frowned.

Eka nodded. "Three's enough."

And what had they really found? No sign of Lintu in either Romania or Greece or any of the countries they visited but, but many spots had that familiar, strange energy connecting to other worlds and they were all associated with earthquakes. Now that they knew the sensation, they'd found the other spots easily, such as in Tokyo or Qeutta, pretty much abandoning their list.

To be fair, she hadn't looked in non-disaster places. Maybe it was in a ton of spots all over the world, but still. And now they were following that same pull, toward what was probably another strange, but dead end, spot.

"You think we'll find an SOSE?"

What? Liney cocked her head as she walked next to Eka.

A small grin spread across Eka's face. "A Spot Of Strange Energy."

I don't know. Liney skipped over her very cool abbreviation like she didn't notice.

Christelle would've giggled.

But the stone is glowing again.

It really was. Liney's stone had glowed each time they'd found another spot, and this time it was almost too bright to look at, especially at night. It also seemed to be a compass, leading them across the landscape to all kinds of abandoned buildings. This time, they were headed over the ridge of a hill to, her guess, another old, forgotten building.

They crested and Eka grinned. It was another abandoned building.

"Nailed it." She started down the side but heard only her footsteps. When she turned, Liney stood frozen at the top, the stone pulsing and glowing in her hand. "Liney?"

This is it. Liney barely whispered.

Eka looked at the building then back at Liney. "What it?"

Where I came…into here. With the others.

"Ohhhh." Eka stared at the dry, scrubby area in front of her, and the tumbling walls of the old building. She sensed it then, an energy, different than the deep space energy they'd found at the other places. Oh, it was here too. In fact, it shown brighter here, especially in the dark night. And different to the Gaian energy that flowed all around them. But there were faint traces of familiar energies. Irida, Lintu, Liney. Somehow, their energy had lingered in this place for all the years since they'd come through.

Eka's mind stopped. "We found it."

She stumbled forward. Where to? Maybe toward the glowing light on the ground, the one that matched Liney's stone. Kneeling in front of the glow she realized it was coming from a stone, unlike the other places. She stared down at it, trying to wrap her head around what she was experiencing. It seemed to be just another stone, but somehow stronger than Liney's. This one was a stone of space, and doors, and travel. Like Liney's story. The stone pulled at Eka, tugging on her magic, drawing her hand toward it. Then her fingers were brushing it and a pulse exploded from it, rushing through her and out around the landscape. Portals flashed through her mind and her body seemed to jump to other places, sensations of greenery, ice, heat, emptiness whizzing by like trees on a highway. Then Eka sagged, her hand dropping from the stone as it quieted.

What just happened?

"Liney…" Eka's call died as a ragged and dirty woman came running from the abandoned building.

"No! What are you doing? They'll find it!" She tackled Eka, then searched around. "How are you doing that?"

"What?" Eka, now laying flat next to the woman could tell through the grim and ragged clothes that her energy may have been dull, but she was a Waker.

"The stone." Then the woman's eye's widened as she stumbled back away from Eka. "What are you?"

You are her. Eka jumped at Liney's voice behind her.

"Oh. My. God." The woman's eyes were gonna pop out of her head if she wasn't careful. "You."

And you. Liney just stared back.

Eka hopped up and found herself turning back and forth between the cryptic conversation. "What's going on."

She was here. The energy person who ran. Liney pointed at the woman. *I saw you when I came through.* Liney stated this flatly. *You were with that man.*

The woman, still backing up, was scanning around her. "With that thing. You were with that thing."

Eka frowned, that thing? "Wait, no. She's not with Lintu."

"Who?" The woman had stopped moving.

"That leachy thing, that steals everyone's energy. She just got stuck here with it."

The woman narrowed her eyes without saying anything, but stopped backing up.

Did we just hit the jackpot? Is this really her, the Waker who was here when they all came through that tear?

"Look, we're just trying to understand what happened. What Lintu wants, really. How to stop him." Eka looked at the stone. "What this has to do with anything." She glanced up at the woman. "I'm guessing you have a great story."

"I…"

Then they all felt it, Eka knew, because everyone froze. Stopped breathing. That oily, cloying cold sent goosebumps and shudders rumbling through her as a shadowed portal swirled open.

No. Both Liney's thought and the woman's whisper came at her as Eka threw up a shield around them. They needed to leave, fast. If she timed it right, she could drop the shield as Liney portaled them out.

"Eka."

The sound grabbed her heart and stopped it's beat. "Ke?" From the swirling shadows, he stepped out. He may be taller, have a beard, look like a man. But there, in front of her, was her brother Ke. She opened her mouth, but her voice failed.

Ke smiled. "Eka, I'm glad we're meeting. I really wanted to before this, but…" He shrugged and spread his arms. "Things happened."

Air rushed into her lungs but her brain was on autopilot. "Ke?"

"There's plenty of time to catch up. I can take you to where I've been."

"Where you've been?" Eka blinked and her brain started up just a little. Ke had came through a Lintu portal. "Ke." She started slowly. "Why did you come through that…thing?"

Ke's eyes. Where was that twinkle she remembered. They looked so…cold.

He took a breath. "It saved me, Eka. When our parents died, it got me out before all those lights…that thing that killed them." Then his face dropped, for a moment. The Ke from their childhood, stared back at her. "I thought you were dead too. That it had killed you."

Her heart broke and she wanted to hug him like she used to. But somehow, he had the story all wrong. He needed to know. "What lights?" Irida's energy flashed in her mind. "Oh. You mean Irida?"

"Oh." His voice chilled. It really sounded like cracking ice. "It has a name."

How did he think that Irida killed their family? Believe that all those years?

"No, Ke, that's wrong."

"Eka, you need to come with me. You don't understand. But I can help you."

He wasn't listening, she had to make him understand. If she could just reach him.

Liney, I've got to talk with him.

Eka, this is bad. Not a good idea. Liney was shaking her head, hard.

I have to. But you'll be safe here. Watch her.

Eka nodded at the woman, who stood transfixed, probably in fear, then turned back to Ke. "I can talk, but nothing happens to these two."

"Deal." Ke smiled. Not really a smile she liked. Should she trust him? He was her brother. But, he also came out of that portal.

Damnit.

All those times he'd helped her with a project, made sand castles, stuck up for her. She couldn't leave him with a lie. Leave him with Lintu.

She slowly dropped the shield and walked forward. This was it, a moment she really hadn't believed could ever happen. A moment she thought was just a fantasy. He watched her, a smile, Ke's smile, growing on his face. This couldn't be real. She slapped herself.

"Ow."

Yep. Real.

Ke frowned briefly.

"Ke, I…"

Then Ke's eyes flickered to the stone. He wanted it. Her feet stopped moving and a tiny, nagging thought erupted in her mind. Crap! She'd led them to this stone, whatever they needed it for. She suddenly knew, in her gut, that she had to get it out of here.

Then, his frown morphed to shock. "No! She's coming with me."

Eka! Liney's scream echoed through her head.

Eka spun just as two more portals started to open, then she glanced back at Ke, who was shouting and running for her. From one of the portals He'e stumbled out, walking in that crazy puppet dance toward the stone. What the hell? The last time she'd seen her crazy, manipulative grandmother was in Hawaii, just before the woman tried to kill her and Lintu took her.

Before she could ponder how He'e was now a Lintu puppet, her gut screamed at her to get that stone. She moved toward it when Wallace stumbled out of the second portal, walking that same unnatural puppet walk and headed toward the woman, pulling her energy into him as he started draining her.

Are you kidding? These two.

She glanced at the Waker woman then the stone. In a split second, she'd decided as she sent an image to Liney then turned to Ke just as he made it to her. "I love you Ke." Then she dissipated, flowing quickly to the woman and Liney as Liney opened a portal and sent them all through it.

Christelle Finds A Crystal

Calling this space a lab was a bit of a stretch, when she looked around. Empty shelves and tables surrounded the lone used table, where the device was spread out with stuff that looked like a little kid had dumped her pockets all around it. One of the two technicians, Solia towered over the jumble, fitting pieces together before sending her uliee through them, examining the results. Her brown skin, white hair, and height always caught Christelle off guard. Despite her quietness, no one would ever miss she her in the room. So opposite of the other tech, Bur. Square, dark, and pale white Ysian hair, he always seemed to blend into the background. Which was weird. Did he have some special gift to disappear? Maybe, until he talked, which always seemed to be when she wanted quiet.

At least they were friendly, which was more than any other Ysian here.

Christelle walked over to the table, across from Solia, and grabbed a few pieces.

"Think today you'll get it?"

Christelle shrugged and grabbed a tiny bellows.

"Christelle thinks she's figured it out." Tanu watched Christelle's hands, glancing at Solia briefly. "Can you imagine if she figures it out? Isamea could really stop that thing."

"Figured it out?" Solia tapped her finger on the table as she studied Christelle's movements.

Christelle nodded. "I was trying to fit these in the right order, to build up the energy to the right amount, but I realized it might be the, uh…frequency?" She shook her head, the right words just didn't exist but she could sense what part of the energy needed adjusting. And it wouldn't be easy. "But I'm just not sure how to get all the frequencies of energy to interact the right way."

"We heard you might have solved the issue with the device." Nor stood at the entrance, arms folded over his large chest.

Christelle turned away from her work and stared. "What? Maybe, I'm just checking out…how did you know?"

Nor ignored her question with his own. "So what's this frequency thing?"

How did he know? A man tumbling, a dropped crystal, flashed through her mind. The guy in the hall.

"What's with all the crystals a lot of the Ysians have?" If he wanted answers, so did she.

Nor tensed and narrowed his eyes at her. "That's none of your business."

Christelle glared at him as she crossed her arms. Who is this guy? "What does that mean?"

"It means," he countered her glare and raised her a flare of uliee. "You do your work and leave the questions to me."

Christelle sent a burst of wind, full of uliee, directly at him, but it fizzled. *Fizzled!* Her uliee was pulled into a crystal around his neck.

"What was that?"

"I said," Nor smirked, and she really, really, really hated smirks, "do your work and no questions."

Christelle took a step forward.

I'll show him questions.

Before she could take the next step, which wasn't really going to be a step, Solia moved between them. "Nor, we'll let you know as soon as we figure anything out. We have to test everything before we're sure it even works."

Nor's energy flared a few times as Christelle's eyes stayed locked on his. Then a knock on her knee dropped her gaze back to Tanu briefly, who shook her head. Christelle huffed and turned back, but Nor was already turning.

"Fine, but inform me of anything you find." Then, the jerk left.

And a murky, muddy film slithered from the doorway and across the walls. "Just in case you were thinking of leaving." The jerk was still there, on the other side of the doorway.

Christelle charged the opening, hitting the slithering, murky boundary, which started to pull at her energy. Pulls that reminded her of Lintu and she froze.

How? He can't…

She couldn't move and that creep loved it. Then hands pulled her back and she blinked at the boundary, and at the jerk on the other side.

"Hope that didn't hurt too much."

Her energy flared, but kinda fizzled again in shock.

"Ah, a bit off."

"Blah, blah, blah. Easy to talk when you're hiding." Tanu stepped in front of Christelle, mimicking a mouth with her hand.

"Shut up, you little…"

"Blah, blah." Tanu hand mimicked.

"Why…"

"Blah." This time she added an eyeroll.

"You'll get that device running." He glared, *again*, then turned and walked away.

Christelle spun around, taking in the oily barrier. "Are you kidding me?" She probably should still feel fear, this stuff was so much like Lintu's energy, but she now all she wanted was to punch something. Or through something. Her uliee pulsed. "I know I can get us out of here."

Solia tapped her shoulder. "Probably, but would it destroy the place?"

Tanu sighed. "Maybe not the effect you want."

Christelle yelled, for just a moment. "What the hell is going on?" She turned to Solia. "And you, you were on his side." She paced and threw up her hands. "Whatever that side is. And where is Isamea!"

"Listen," Solia lowered her voice to barely a whisper, "you have to trust me."

"Trust you? Right now I don't even know if I trust myself." Christelle really didn't know what she was about to do, so yeah.

"Please, whisper." Solia walked over to an empty shelf and laid her hand over it, her uliee flowing across it. Then the rock rolled back and Solia pulled something from a little cavity which quickly disappeared again.

Christelle strode over, Tanu close behind. Solia was holding a crystal, a light green one, in her hand. "What is it? Why did my energy get sucked in to the one Nor had?"

Solia held up her free hand. "I thought we'd have more time, but we've run out."

"More time?" Tanu joined the conversation.

Solia took a deep breath and seemed to nod to herself. "I'm trusting you both to understand. Not betray us."

"Us?" Christelle could only guess one person she might be talking about.

"I've called Bur, we've got to leave now." Solia laid the crystal flat against the wall and whispered something. Slowly, almost imperceptibly, the murkiness started flowing into the crystal. "We stayed behind, pretended to support Isamea, when the others fled. But, you seem about to have a break through and we can't let them be the ones who control an upgraded device, so we've got to leave. Now."

Fled? Support Isamea? Leave now? Now she had more questions.

"But…" Tanu started but Solia interrupted.

"No time, grab the device. Bur is waiting."

Christelle crossed her arms. "I know my mom is a bit…intense and this place is kind of crazy." She watched as the last of the energy slipped into the crystal. "And I was just trapped by an jerk." Who she would punch. "But, I don't know you or these people you want us to go to. People that oppose my mom."

"It's your grandparents."

A familiar pang of loss swept through her.

My grandparents?

She didn't even know her grandparents, thanks to her lost childhood. And she definitely didn't know Solia, she could be lying about a connection with them. But, Solia had been friendly, unlike the others. And this place was crazy.

But what if Solia was helping a group even worse than this? Or even Lintu? Christelle shook her head. She didn't feel anything like *that* coming off Solia, and Christelle could handle herself in most situations. And, what if her grandparents had left for a reason?

"Christelle, please, we only have a small window before someone notices what we're doing. We have to go now."

"Fine." She grabbed the device's bag and shoved everything in. Not that she couldn't get this stuff later, but Solia seemed adamant they couldn't leave it. "But keep explaining what is happening."

Solia peered around the now clear opening, then motioned them to follow. "I'll let your grandparents tell you everything. Right now, we need to slip out before anyone notices."

They headed down the hall, toward what Christelle guessed was the marina. The hall was eerily quiet as they sneaked down it. Was it too quiet? She couldn't tell, the place had so few people, but there always seemed to be an echo of feet down some hall, right? Now she wasn't sure.

They shuffled to the wall and started to open the portal, when footsteps, many footsteps, crept up on them. Christelle turned to find Nor with a contingent of soldiers, in the hallway. At least in her mind ten or more was a contingent. And they were definitely soldiers, all wearing a murky crystal. She must have guessed something was up, because she wasn't shocked at that. What did shock her was Tanu, moving to stand with Nor's group.

Then, Bur was shoved from the back of the contingent and he fell near Solia. "Well done, Tanu." Was that a perma-smirk on Nor's stupid face?

"Shut up Nor." Tanu glared at him, then met Christelle's eyes. And sagged.

"Tanu?" Gravity gripped Christelle's heart. Why had Tanu alerted Nor. Christelle wasn't sure betrayal was the right word. Whose side was she on? She didn't know. But she should be able to leave when she wanted. And she had no idea what her mother would think of all this. But that prick, Nor, shouldn't control her. So 'why' was all Christelle could think to ask.

"Isamea saved me. From that thing, Lintu." Tanu's eyes were wet. "I can't betray her."

"Loyalty is rare." Nor nodded.

"Shut up." Tanu, Solia, and Christelle chimed in together.

"You don't know this is what my mother wants." Christelle said.

Or I want.

"But she wanted you here. To fix the device, which will help her finally kill that thing." Tanu seemed to be pleading. "Please Christelle, you have to help her."

Tanu had almost died, Christelle could understand the fear, the pain, in that moment, then the relief when help came. Tanu's trust and loyalty to Isamea made sense. But as she looked around, Christelle finally decided that

Isamea hadn't earned *her* trust or loyalty. She wanted her mother's love, had seen a glimpse of it, and she would find a way to reach that love. But it wouldn't happen here. There wasn't any warmth or love in this place any longer. She'd have to connect with Isamea somewhere else, on neutral ground.

Christelle took a breath. "Sorry, but I'm leaving."

"I don't think so." Nor signaled the group and Christelle froze. Shadowy energy snaked toward them, this time in full force. And she knew that energy, it was just like Lintu's. What were they doing?

Christelle instinctively blew energy at it, but Solia and Bur had no instinct and the energy slid in and started to drain them, tear them up.

"Your energy can't stop this. Just give up and we'll end it." Nor's voice was grating on her soul.

"Stop hurting them!" Tanu hit Nor, but two soldiers pulled her off. "Christelle! Please!"

Then the Solia and Bur started screaming and Christelle sent energy to block those murky streams, giving Solia and Bur a moment of no pain. But she knew she didn't have forever. Her energy was vast but it couldn't stop them, and the stupid device wasn't even functioning yet. Then she noticed the soldiers were spreading out, probably testing what she was capable of in this situation. She could hold off a few, but she wasn't sure how many streams of energy she could manage.

"Give up, Christelle." Nor's nails-on-chalkboard voice grated across her body and she rolled her eyes toward the rock wall then glared at him. If only she could punch him once, it might be worth staying.

Oh, wait. Behind the soldiers, the wall of rock loomed. And wedged in the craggy surface were pebbles.

She briefly glanced at the walls again, then sent a small bit of the energy she could spare down her foot and underground to the wall behind them. She couldn't let them know or they might block her. Slowly, she rolled a small rock off the wall, trying only to look at it from the corner of her eye.

"Christelle, how much longer can you keep this up? Your friends need help."

Her heart stopped and she glanced down at them, then remembered the pebble.

Damnit!

She couldn't see it. Had it fallen? She could dislodge another one, but time was running out. Solia and Bur were already torn up some and she couldn't let them loose any more uliee. And the soldiers were creeping closer, feeling braver as she was countering their moves. Because she couldn't counter all of them. Then, from behind the soldiers, Tanu picked up the pebble.

Double damn!

Nor looked behind him at Tanu, then at Christelle, frowning. "She isn't your friend, she can't help you."

Tanu looked over at Solia and Bur then back at Nor and winced. Then she sighed and closed her palm, saying nothing. She wasn't ratting Christelle out.

Christelle sent another tiny stream of energy underground and up the rock wall, searching for a pebble. But the surface suddenly seemed so clean.

What the hell?

A soldier made a lunge at her and she threw a wind at him, but it only pushed him back a few feet and a splash hit her nose and she realized she was sweating and shaking. She had so much more energy but her body didn't seem capable of channeling at a higher rate. Then she realized that all the soldiers had crystals and they were all draining her uliee.

Oh crap.

Out of the corner of her eye, Christelle saw Tanu, still behind the soldiers, hold up the pebble she'd found. Without thinking, Christelle took a shaky breath and sent another tiny stream of energy underground to Tanu, picking up the pebble. And whipping it at the head of each soldier in turn, hitting them with a force that cracked their skulls and sent them down. The initial noise had the others looking around, then dropping, until, with the smirk replaced by surprise, the rock slammed into Nor's skull and he joined the others on the floor.

Damn, that felt good.

Christelle was breathing pretty heavily, maybe not all from exertion. Around her, the few bodies lay piled, but she could make out the ins and outs of shallow breath.

And Tanu behind them. "Christelle I didn't mean for anyone to get hurt." She looked at the bodies, "You…"

Anger, sadness, bitterness, betrayal. Maybe some of those, or all of those, animated Christelle right now. She just wanted out of this place.

She turned without speaking and helped the unconscious Solia and Bur up with a bit of wind, not even looking back at Tanu. She didn't know what to say. Then she stumbled into the cold water, wrapping the other two in air, not sure they would breath right under water, given their state. She scanned the area and the dying coral boats, all waiting to ride out. Great. She had no idea how to pilot them or where to go.

Then she heard the song. Fin! But there were more. She swam to the opening from the marina, pulling the others along and as she came out the opening, Fin and four other whales waited, Ysians beside them. She froze, until she realized she'd never seen these Ysians and they were exploding with uliee. They were just as she'd imagined all Ysians to be, before she came to Ys.

Christelle, we're here to help. One of the unknown Ysians mindspoke with her. *Solia called us.*

Should she trust them? She glanced back at the portal to Ys.

Well, I'm not going back there.

She turned to the floating group and swam toward them, pulling Solia and Bur behind her. She was exhausted, ready to unload her passengers onto anyone else and sleep for a hundred years. As the Ysians took over her unconscious passengers, she really hoped she'd made the right choice.

Thirteen Eka Knocks On A Door

Eka stumbled through the portal, hoping her multiple-portal jump had thrown Ke and the others off. Liney had sent them to a remote island she must have gone to at one time, but neither one of them felt comfortable staying and Eka thought they'd be better off splitting up. So she'd taken the unconscious woman through a dozen portals then headed to the one spot she was confident was isolated and unknown, for now, the barn. She dropped the woman in hay and breathed in the familiar smell of the wobbly structure.

Still empty.

Eka examined the woman who was still out, but didn't seem to be injured from He'e or Wallace.

Why was it always those two? "Doesn't Lintu have anyone else?"

Eka jumped at a rustling outside and she crawled to the edge of the loft opening. Squinting in the minute moonlight, she just made out a cat crawling around in the grass outside. Her whole body released the sudden tension but her mind still whirled with possibilities. Were they safe now? How *had* Ke known she was at that last spot at that moment? This woman seemed to think activating that stone would bring them, but none of the other stones brought Lintu's people. Was it because the stone was whole and sent out a stronger signal they were waiting for?

A slight throb in her hand reminded her of the sensation of space, doors, distant worlds, a whisper, and a pulsing through her body when she touched the stone. For just a moment, she'd been in so many places, spread across space, before collapsing back into herself. Did Christelle feel that kind of connection to all the Gaian energy?

When would she ever be able to ask Christelle anything again?

Throbbing grabbed her attention and she shook out her hand. What had the stone done to her? And what was that pulse of energy that came from it.

"Maybe they sensed the energy." She mumbled, looking down at the woman. "If that's true, guess we're safe. For now." It's not like she saved the stone from Ke.

Ke.

"What happened to you?" He was alive, but he was with Lintu. How could he do that? "Ke, why would you believe Lintu saved you?"

Of course there wasn't an answer. And her memories had just recently come back. Maybe he lost his, and Lintu fed him that story, He'e agreeing. But, he must've seen what was going on now. Right? All the killings? And the weirdest thing, why had Lintu taken him then tried to take her? And what could they have to do with that stone?

During the chaos, she'd seen a brief moment of the real Ke, *her* brother. He was still in there and she had to try to reach him, someone had to care. She'd been lucky, had Sema and Win growing and he had Lintu. She shivered at what he went through. And if she could break through, she'd have her brother back. And he'd know everything that's going on with Lintu, including a way to stop him.

"Great plan, but how in Hades are you going to do this?"

How would she get Ke alone, without He'e, Wallace, or Lintu. It would have to be away from Lintu's place, wherever that was. She knew Lintu wanted her, so maybe Ke would show up if she 'accidentally' let him know where she was, like this last time. But how could she do that? Last time she had that stone.

Okay, but I don't have it. I…

Liney's memory stone.

Mele flew in, their connection stronger each day. As he zipped around her head, she sent an image of Liney and her need to bring Liney back. Mele chittered acknowledgement, then shot off in search of the elusive off-worlder.

Eka jumped through the loft door and into the air, then opened a portal right under her. And fell from the ceiling onto some hay. After a few days, there was no Ke and no Lintu, woot woot. They hadn't found her hiding spot. But there was no Liney either.

Where are you Mele?

A soft snore floated across the loft and Eka shook her head. That woman, whoever she was, was still unconscious and needed help. Maybe it was safe to get help, but who could she ask? She had no idea where Christelle was. Who else was there?

A flash of Jason healing Brigg stopped her. Of course. But did she want to go back to the ship? A glance at her unconscious companion answered her question.

Come on Liney, where are you?

She really couldn't wait any longer. Sighing, she kneeled next to the sleeping body and portaled them out of the barn.

Vines, entwined into the shape of a round door, loomed in front of Eka. It was actually pretty small, but somehow it seemed so large, and her hand lay at her side, not knocking. Sunlight almost ensured they were alone in this area of the ship,with most of the Wakers asleep.

It's okay, no one followed you here.

Eka took a deep breath and rapped loudly. Very loudly.

Shuffling followed muffled voices before the door creaked open. "Eka?" Jason rubbed his eyes, squinting.

"Uh, hey ? I need a little help." Eka nodded toward the body at her feet and Jason's eyes stopped squinting and exploded.

"What? Who is that?" He popped his head out and looked around. "What's going on?"

"We were attacked."

"Shit." He lifted up the unconscious woman and floated her inside, gesturing for Eka to follow.

Ping sat on the bed, arms crossed as he watched their little parade dump into the room, silent as usual.

"So," Jason rolled his hand impatiently, waiting for a story.

"Can you fix her?" Eka asked.

Jason huffed as he bent down next to her. "Story."

"I found her?" Maybe answering with questions wasn't the right direction.

"Eka." Ping finally joined the conversation.

"Fine." Eka paced. "I was looking for information, anything really." She had been, right. Trying to find information to help. NOT find Ke.

"Hello, Eka." Jason eyed her from beside the woman, pulling her out of her thoughts.

"Um, yeah. So, I started with that story and found a pattern of disasters. Natural disasters." No need to include Liney in this. "And there were stones, well parts of them, with this strange energy at these places and the last place, well, the stone sort of went off, and this woman," she pointed at the body, "came from no where and freaked out. Then…" Ke showed up. "Lintu's minions arrived and attacked. And we ran."

Accurate. Enough.

The two men looked at each other then back at Eka. "I don't really know where to start." Jason gaped at her.

"Stones." Ping stated.

"Okay, stones." Jason agreed.

Eka shrugged, shaking her head. "I don't know. I was just looking for a natural disaster, around the time of a big war but there weren't many, so I expanded the search. And let me tell you, none of these places were easy to get to." Dematerializing into trains, airplanes, cars, and that one wagon train. Why was that even on the road?

"Eka!" Jason snapped his fingers.

"Uh, so yeah, these weird stones, or pieces of them, were buried at each site. And they had really strange traces of energy. And at that last place, there was a whole stone." A ghostly throb in her hand sent a tingle of vast space and infinite places washing through her. Like whisper, or a call.

"Okay, this is getting ridiculous." Exasperation exploded from Jason. "Eka, just finish the story!"

She rubbed her hand while trying to shake off the sensation. "Um, I think the last place was where it all started. Where Lintu first came through some sort of tear between universes."

"What!" Both men nearly shouted.

"Yeah. This woman was there when we, when I got there and tried to stop me from, I don't know, activating the stone. And it had a weird thing, like doors to other worlds. But before she could say anything, the minions showed up and I grabbed her. But they hurt her before I could get her out and she hasn't woken in a few days. I think she knows what's going on, what the stone's all about and why Lintu is here."

Jason sighed. "Okay, I think my head needs a break." He looked down. "I'll do what I can but I haven't tried healing recently. Not since Christelle left."

Eka knelt next to him. "Just do what you can. Christelle upgraded you and you and Ping are the only ones I know who might be able to help her."

Ping joined them, without comment, and placed Jason's hand on the body, under his. Their collective uliee flowed into the broken bits of the woman's, pulling on strands, adding others, doing the dance Eka had seen with Christelle. They were almost naturals.

As the last strands wove together, the woman stirred. She blinked a number of times, seeming to try and focus, then her head jerked around, taking in everyone and she bolted up. Then stumbled.

"It's okay." Jason held up his hands. "You were hurt and we helped. You're safe in an airship."

Her spooked-looking eyes darted around the room, between them, then she seemed to believe she might be safe as her shoulders sagged and she slumped back to the floor.

"How?" Was all she managed.

"We ran. It's been a few days but they didn't seem to follow." Eka blurted. "I couldn't heal you but I brought you here because they could."

She examined Eka, her eyes widening a bit before she truly took in her surroundings. "He has the stone?"

Eka sighed and nodded.

Suddenly, the world seemed to slam into the woman as her head dropped. "It doesn't matter anymore. He has it."

"What does the stone do?" Jason asked, slowly sitting next to Ping, back on the bed's edge.

She stared at her hands, turning them over and over. Then she seemed to start at a random place in her story. "Our parents were latents, never crossed over to Wakers." She glanced at Jason and Ping and sighed. "They were so confused, but they lived in a little town in Spain, so they hid what they saw from others." She fisted and unfisted her hands. "Those Asleep would have killed them if they knew. Then we were born. Leonardis and Leana." A brief smile flitted across her face. "Twin names. Funny that." Then, her face shifted, all mirth gone. "All our gifts were right there, ready to use. In plain sight for that whole freak of a town to see." Her eyes squeezed shut, chin quivering. "Our parents saved us, but they didn't make it."

Her words floated in the silent room until they drifted away, leaving nothing.

A deep breath later, she was staring at her hands again. "An air group, like this one, took us in, taught us, saved us. I thought we were happy. But," she shook her head. "Leonardis grew to hate how we all had to hide, grew to hate the Awake and started believing we could have a place of our own. He tried to convince others it was possible. A piece of the world that belonged to us. But when no one would listen, except me, he disappeared. He was gone so long without any news, I thought he'd died. And when he came back, it was like he was…different, crazed. He had stories no one else knew. Old stories, ancient stories telling of ways to travel to other worlds and that Wakers had once traveled with others, from other universes. That there were special places here on earth that they traveled from. He said he'd learned it in Ys, from the Keeper. I thought he was just making it up, maybe from wanting some type of escape to be true." Leana starred at the wall, like the story was playing out in front of her and she wanted to capture all the details. "I told him they were just stories, not real and he got so angry, as if by not believing I betrayed him."

She stared for a while at her hands and Eka understood Jason and Pings' frustration. "Was that what it was like listening to my story?" She whispered.

They both rolled their eyes at her. "Shush."

Leana continued as if nothing had happened. "I thought he'd give up, when no one listened. I told him he was chasing fantasies. But he went looking for these places anyway. This time, I decided to go with him. I couldn't lose my only family." She wiped her face lightly. "That's when we found the stones. The first one was so…unexpected. Such strange energy.

Like something in my lighter uliee. And he was so excited…at first. Then frustrated. Nothing he did affected it, it just sat there, dreaming it's dream."

Eka shuddered. That stone did seem like a dreaming stone.

"Nothing happened until I touched it." She dropped her head in her hands. "I shouldn't have, but I just wanted to get rid of it, hide it so he'd let go. But…I saw it. The other places through it. Other worlds." She suddenly starred at them, one after the other. "It was real and I started to believe, maybe we *could* find another home."

"Without Gaia's energy?" Jason interrupted with one of a million questions they could've asked.

Leana shook her head. "It was just…hope. We didn't really think about that. Or anything really, we were just so excited and we started experimenting to get it to work, to reveal it's secrets. We learned the stone needed lighter uliee and mine wasn't enough so we recruited others. The more lighter uliee we pumped into it, the closer we felt it opening. Like a door."

Eka almost nodded.

"Then," Leana unfocused again, maybe watching an internal movie. "The first explosion happened and so many died. Asleep, Wakers, all the other creatures, even bits of the land. I wasn't there that first time, but it went through me and I knew. Somehow Leonardis survived. He wouldn't say but I think…" she took a deep breath. "I think he knew what might happen. I think he…wasn't there when it blew. On purpose." She started crying, then beat her hand into the bed. "He promised that was it. No more experiments so I went back to our air group, thinking he'd join." She shook her head. "He said he needed to explore other options, but he lied. He found other stones, because that first stone was broken. He tried again and again but each one ended in an explosion. And rumors of what those explosions really were, started spreading. No lighters would help, so…he took them. And I couldn't find him until it was too late, after the explosions. Until, the last time."

"Something worked." Eka whispered.

Leana nodded at her. "He had enough lighters, I guess. I was closer this time and was there when it opened, hiding on the outside, looking in. I just didn't know what to do, thought I could rush in when I had some kind of plan." She shuddered. "But it wasn't the stone opening a door. It was forced and ugly and ripped, like my brother." She barely whispered that last part. "And energy came through, like the stone energy, then disappeared." She glanced at Eka who shook her head. Leana paused a moment then continued. "Then Lintu came through. It ran through the whole space, sucking away…" She shivered and her voice dropped. "Taking all the energy from every Waker in the room until Leonardis was all that was left. My brother tried to run, but it was just hazy shadows at that time and expanded into him." Her breath caught and she just stared for a few moments.

Flashes of the island back in Manatee Isles and Lintu's hazy form attacking them sent shudders through her, but then the image of Sema turning to ash punched her in the gut and Eka mimiced Leana as she stared at a wall and shut away these events in the back of her emotions for another time.

"And I watched as that thing, Lintu, took over my brother and he wasn't there anymore." Leana's story jerked Eka back to the present. "It looked like him, but I watched his light go out and I knew he was gone. I just stood there and did nothing for him." She shook her head. "I couldn't even move as I saw it, Leonardis, Lintu look at me through the window and move my way, like a puppet." She was starting at the wall until this moment. She turned to Eka. "Then, this explosion of colors, and a burst of deep space uliee lit up the room and the rip closed just as I felt others like Lintu trying to get through. It rammed right into my brother…that thing and they, I can only describe it as fighting. Somehow, Lintu got a way with those lights chasing him. I don't know how long I stood there before the tremors started. All the others were dead, there was no one else to save, so I ran out. When the killings started again, I went back, hoping I could keep that thing away from the stone. From opening up the rip again and letting in the others."

"There others." Jason stated, strangely quiet.

"There were other shadows, like that thing. I think they would have come through if that colorful energy hadn't shut it down. And now, the stone's been activated again. And that thing, that used to be my brother, has it."

"What?" Jason and Ping must be timing their answers. "How? What happened."

"Ask her." Leanna pointed at Eka.

Eka backed up. "I…I don't know."

"You're energy, like lighter uliee, activates the stone. The stone recognizes it." Leanna continued. "But it reacted more than to any lighter I've seen. And how did you know that man. The one who wanted the stone?"

Everyone was staring at Eka now.

"Uh, I really need to go."

"Eka." Jason shook his head. "What is going on with you? The stone? Lintu?"

"I…I don't know, really. Just, let her stay here. And protect any lighters you can." Eka turned and fled out the door then portaled into the rigging. They would never believe Ke was still himself, she barely believed it. But she had to try to reach him and she needed to find Liney.

Just then Mele fluttered around her, followed by Fluffy and Liney. "Holy cannoli, where've you been?"

Liney shrugged.

"Hey, I didn't see them again, I think we're safe at the barn." Without waiting for an answer, Eka portaled over, Liney arriving a second later with Mele and Fluffly.

Did you get the stone? Liney asked very quietly.

Eka shook her head. "I saved the woman, but they got the stone."

Liney sagged, something Eka'd never seen her do.

"Listen, I really need to use those stone bits you collected."

Why?

"I have a plan but, you need to keep an open mind." Eka smiled, kind of. Well, more a forced grin.

Oh. Even Liney knew what that meant.

Christelle Turns On Some Lights

They'd traveled for a while, Fin and the other whales carrying them. Well, time was a bit abstract at this point. Maybe it'd been just a little while, after all there wasn't any drastic changes in the scenery which Christelle noticed. But they weren't as deep in the ocean, with coral surrounding them and warmer, lighter water, so, yeah different. She lay on some sand, tiny, bright anemones swaying with a light current, reminding her of the forest canopy in Hawaii.

What had happened back in Ys?

Tanu, standing with those Ysians, betraying her, played havoc with her memories, tangling them and making her wonder if Tanu was a spy the whole time.

And then there was Isamea. Would she have been okay with everything that happened? Would she have accepted her people trying to force Christelle to stay, threatening her when she tried to leave?

Hadn't she seen glimpses of her mother, the one from those faint, childhood memories, in Isamea's eyes? The memories where her mother had cleaned a skinned knee, had comforted her when she was scared, and had played hide and seek all those times. There were those moments that every bit of Christelle believed her real mother was still part of Isamea and she just had to reach that part again.

Now here she was, hiding out from the one person, the one place, that she'd been looking for since she'd rediscovered her Waker life.

"Christelle!"

She turned at her grandmother's voice, a smile creeping across her face as she sat up. She never really thought about these other grandparents. She'd probably met them once, but none of those memories had surfaced, so now she had a chance to create new memories with new family and hopefully they'd be wonderful memories.

That's one good thing about this whole mess. That and understanding these weird, water noises.

In her head, she ran the lip movements of her grandmother against the sound of her name, sound that was almost like dolphins or even some whales.

How can I understand them? I mean, they're speaking underwater. I'm speaking underwater.

It didn't make any sense, at least in her head. But it felt right in her body, just like breathing in water.

"We thought you'd disappeared!" Her grandfather swam up next to her, her grandmother close behind. He took her hand, turning it over before checking the other hand and her face. "You're okay."

"Jan, leave the girl be. She's fine." Her grandmother shook her head. "Honestly, she just was gone a minute."

"Don't pretend you were okay, Sashine. You were the first one out to look." He turned to her, crossing his arms.

Sashine huffed, then sat next to Christelle. Jan floated next to them, arms still crossed, until Christelle patted the area on her other side and he quickly plopped down next to her. If she didn't know they were her grandparents, Christelle would swear they were college age kids on holiday.

"You always did have my chin." Jan smiled at her.

"Well, she has my hair."

"Everyone here has your hair." Jan shook his head.

Christelle almost giggled, hiding it under a cough. Their banter seemed so normal in this wackadoo moment she'd tumbled into.

"Well, she's a beautiful girl." Sashine smiled at her again.

"Thanks, Grandma?" That one word seemed weird and awkward, she'd only known Sashine for a short bit. But her grandmother swept her up in a hug and after a brief moment of tension, relaxed into the comforting arms, finally hugging her back. She really did have more family.

"Yes, she looks just like Isamea." Jan winked at Christelle but his smile dropped as Christelle's body stiffened again.

"Jan!" Sashine released Christelle and she swatted Jan from across Christelle's stiff form.

"Oh honey, I didn't mean to bring her up." Jan's mouth squeezed into a thin line for a moment.

"Uh, why don't we head in. Everyone wants to celebrate you joining us." Sashine floated upright, holding out her hand.

"I don't know." Christelle sighed. All her churning emotions could spill out in front of everyone.

Sashine glanced at Jan. "If you don't mind, everyone really needs a pick me up, something to get their spirits back. This could be it."

"I guess." Christelle took Sashine's hand and floated up, Jan following. Helping out wouldn't be the worst thing. She could always wallow later.

The coral room emanated life, so much more than the sad boats back in Ys. This coral was alive and thriving. Maybe the Ysians here were outcasts from the home they'd created, but they were far more alive with uliee than any back in Ys. Ys was dying, but it's true people weren't.

Maybe Ys is wherever the people are.

Whatever was going on, this moment and place seemed the most natural to her. She'd even donned a strange, multi-colored top and silvery pants that seemed to be made of the sea itself. With these on, she slid through the water like a colorful, fishy disco ball.

She ran her hand along the anemones and a little purple fish even allowed her to brush her fingers along it's side. Since they were always submerged here, the Ysians had managed to talk the microscopic, glowing creatures into creating pockets of light. She wiggled her finger in one of these pockets along the coral wall and it flare briefly before calming back into a bluish glow. A chittering resonated through her; the little creatures didn't enjoy her gigantic swishing of their space.

"Sorry."

She swam out, taking in all the small rooms grown out of the coral. A beautiful village. Ysian children swam in and out of the coral, playing with the sea life and each other. In the center of it all, a large group was gathering, with hundreds of the little pockets of free-floating light bobbing amongst the crowd. Tables of rock jutted out of the sand and there were strange stacks of what seemed like food. Maybe everyone was indulging tonight, eating for pleasure and joy.

Had Ys been this warm and alive? Before her mother came back?

At one of the tables, her grandparents hovered, almost sitting, but without any chairs. They waved her over and she slid in between them as they made room for her.

"Isn't this wonderful?" Sashine grinned, something dangling from her mouth. Was it a piece of seaweed?

Jan tapped his mouth while looking at her and she quickly stuffed it her mouth, laughing as the thing disappeared. Jan shook his head, but smiled as he squeezed Christelle's shoulder. "We're glad you're here. Wasn't sure you'd come out."

Christelle took in the gathering. Smiles, which hadn't been on display at all back in Ys and had been tentative here, now lit all the faces. Everyone seemed relaxed, not on alert. Almost as if her arrival and a celebration signaled safety. Maybe she *could* do something besides mope while she was here. "Glad I came." Her smile went through her.

"Great!" Sashine held up more of the slimy delights. "Want some?"

Christelle's stomach lurched. "Uh, no. Thanks." Sashine shrugged and dug in, Jan eating just a few. Seems like both her grandmothers liked to eat. An image of Shirley at dinner floated through her mind and she suddenly missed the smile of the ostentatious woman she loved so much. These new grandparents were wonderful, and Christelle imagined she'd grow to love them, but she could use the comfort of someone that had been there all her life. Someone that had held her through all the hard times, someone she deeply trusted and could relax around, like Shirley, or her Dad. Even Pekoi had worked his way into that unwavering loyalty category.

Chattering from other groups shook her out of her reverie.

Focus on now. You haven't lost the others, you're just gaining new people to love.

She chanted this mantra as she took in the larger area.

At the expansive, community table, families jostled with each other in the way she guessed families did, when they were so familiar with each other they could finish sentences, anticipate a tickle, even know which dish to pass. Would she ever have that with any of her family? She had once, kind of, with her father. Although she knew now he'd probably been depressed all those years. And she had thought that was the kind of relationship she'd shared with Aunt Anise and Uncle Ben, but…her heart hurt at their memories now, the anger long gone.

Well, there's Grams, Ben, Eka, and Pekoi.

But they seemed so far away.

Then, there was her mother.

She'd had at least a small childhood with her, shouldn't there be something left. There had to be.

"Christelle." Sashine placed her hand on Christelle's arm. "You're thinking about her."

Her grandmother's touch reminded her she could have something wonderful with these two people. They were so happy to see her and she'd forgiven everyone for her lost childhood since her own mistakes humbled her back in Hawaii.

"Christelle?" Sashine furrowed her eyebrows and brought Christelle out of her thoughts.

She shrugged and rubbed her cheek. "I guess Mom's on my mind. And other things."

"You can't hide that look. Jan always gets that look when he's thinking of her."

Jan glanced at Christelle then at Sashine. "That's the look?"

Sashine nodded.

"Ohhhh. No wonder you always know." He narrowed his eyes at her. "Why don't you get that look?"

"A Keeper thing." She waggled her eyebrows.

"Keeper?"

"Your grandmother, well…" Jan cocked his head and scrunched his mouth to the side for a moment. "Strangely, both your grandmothers are a bit special. Sashine is the living memory of all Wakers."

Christelle stared at the woman before her. A living memory? "What does that mean?"

Sashine swallowed her latest bite and cleared her throat. "I have all the memories since Wakers began." She ran her hand from her head to her toes.

"As if I lived them. Every sight, sound, sensation."

"But, what, where, how…?" Christelle's vocabulary recall failed.

"How does my mind not explode?"

Yes. Not explode. Sounds right.

Christelle nodded.

Sashine shrugged. "Just doesn't. I may remember thousands of years of all Wakers, but it's packed away until I need it. And I don't understand everything they came to understand, just can recall what they experienced." She leaned in. "Wouldn't want to know some of the things Wakers' came to believe, trust me." She tapped her head then sat up. "Some things are better off mysteries."

"Mysteries keep life alive, if you ask me." Jan bobbed his head at Christelle.

"I, I don't know what to say. Everything?"

Sashine nodded. "Everything. But only Waker stuff."

Maybe she should leave this for when she could form a coherent question. "So, you mentioned Grams being special?"

"Shirley? She's a Seer. Those are pretty rare, although there's only one Keeper at any time." Jan reached over and squeezed Sashine's shoulder. "And this time around it's my Sashine."

"And you, our Uon. We're quite the power couple." Sashine grinned back. Then they both looked around the gathering and broke into laughter. "For Ysians in hiding."

Isamae's few soft moments flashed through Christelle's memory.

"On no, the look's back." Jan patted Christelle's hand again.

"I just don't understand? I remember her laughing." Seemed the crazy past year and past moments were catching up with Christelle and thoughts were jumping out of her, and into the world, without rhyme or reason. At least none she could catch.

"Ah, honey. Your mother has the best laugh in the world. Starts right here." Sashine tapped her stomach. "And wiggles and whirls it's way out, exploding in a madcap frenzy."

Jan nodded. "Grabs everyone around her and shakes them up till their own laughs escape. Pretty soon, everyone is holding their stomachs…"

"And sides."

"Yes." He laughed a bit.

The image they conjured almost had Christelle laughing right then and she could remember moments like that as a child.

"I miss that so much." Jan sighed.

"Oh, Jan. We all do."

"So." Christelle stared between them. They had to have an answer, because that laugh was no where in Ys. "Where's her laugh now? And why is she so distant from Dad?"

Sashine sighed this time. "So much happened to her, because of those attacks."

"And we had no idea," Jan jumped in, "what they were going to do to you. If only we'd known, we could have stopped it."

"That's true." Sashine nodded agreement. "But we can't change the past." She stared up. "At least, I don't think we can." After a brief moment she shook out her head. "We only learned after your family came back to stay with us. The story Isamea told us shocked everyone. She begged us to change the memory wipe." Sashine almost seemed to go back to that moment, her face a momentary poster for heartbreak.

"We wanted to." Jan jumped in. "But the only one who could change it was the one who made the wipe, Anise. We pleaded with Shirley, but she couldn't convince Anise to change her mind."

"Well, Gaia could have changed it, but she was so quiet. No one could get in touch with her."

Christelle knew that part of the story.

"Your mother swore she'd track down the danger, destroy it, show Anise none of you were a danger. You're father hid in the Asleep world and your mother went searching in that same world. They thought if they never used their uliee, that thing couldn't find them while she looked. And we really wanted to see you, but, unlike in Hapton, there was no way to hide our world from you. So we had to stay out of your life." Sashine's voice broke on the last bit and she grasped Christelle's hand fiercely.

Christelle had never thought how all of this affected them. To be fair, she hadn't really thought about her mother's family at all. Her dad had done a marvelous job keeping her distracted from all family questions, avoiding them with emergencies. She'd really thought her Dad was clumsy and incompetent.

"We didn't see her for a long time, no contact at all." Jan wiped at his cheeks. "We would send people out, under the guise of training the other Wakers in the wake of the attacks. But no one ever had news of her. Until…"

"Until she came back." Sashine's shoulders squared. "She was different."

"She was still Isamea." Jan added.

"She was harder. The laugh was gone. She was actually advocating for Asleep style military training. Weaponizing our gifts."

"We've always had to prepare for a fight using our gifts." Jan jumped in.

Sashine shook her head at him. "We've never wanted to use it to wipe out the Asleep and control the other Wakers."

Christelle looked quickly between them. "She wanted to do all that?"

Jan's shoulders slumped, but Sashine continued, a slight narrowing of her eyes seemed aimed at no one present. "I love my daughter, but she came back so like others I can remember, so rigid and walled off. She wasn't even looking to get back to Jake or you anymore, like her goals had changed. And when we disagreed, she started stirring up our community with fear, telling all the others that Gaia had abandoned them and that the Asleep were dangerous, that non-Ysian Wakers were dangerous, that we needed to take charge of the world if we were going to stop the attacks. The world needed to follow her lead if we were going to ever be safe again."

What had happened to her mother?

"But…I saw her, the old her. She still cares."

Jan nodded. "She is still there. She just needs time."

Sashine raised her hands and spread them out. "How much time do we have? She and the others, have lost most of their gifts, Ys is dying, and she knows how to steal energy, even uliee, and store it in the crystals. She's dangerous."

"Mom is stealing energy?" Christelle's stomach churned.

Like Lintu. No, that can't…why…

"I think I saw those crystals in Ys. Some of the Ysians were wearing them." Christelle frowned, then her whole body lightened for a moment. "But Mom never had one."

Sashine sighed, her tirade seemed to deflate at the new direction. "She's the one that showed those *Ysians* what they were and how to use them."

"What?" This time Christelle's whole body went numb.

Jan sighed next. "We used to store energy, energy others gave us, for our cities."

"Cities?" Christelle's words were starting to come back, but this whole exchange wasn't proving that.

Sashine smiled half-heartedly. "Before there were Asleep, Wakers had beautiful, living cities. We were part of the world, our energy feeding all the life so that it flourished. But there were so few of us that we started keeping some of Gaia's energy and some energy from around us, in crystals so the cities could run without constant input from us." Sashine seemed to be somewhere else.

"When Asleep took some crystals and started to enslave the world, we fought." Jan stepped in. "And then our world was split forever. Us, hiding, helping the world as much as we could, the few remaining Asleep multiplying and, well, not helping the world much at all. But we kept the crystals, and ourselves, away from any Asleep this time. We hid those crystals so well that only a few Wakers knew about them."

"I made the mistake of getting involved with a latent that had found his way back to us." Sashine seemed smaller all of a sudden. "I…thought he loved us. I told him stories, old stories. And he asked so many questions. I really thought he just wanted to know our world. But…"

"But he found the hidden crystals and experimented on stealing energy. Killed our son, among others."

"I had an uncle?"

Talking better now.

Sashine dropped her head in her hands and Jan squeezed her shoulder.

"When our world had finally stopped him and the others, we decided to hide the crystals, even from other Wakers." Jan almost whispered. "But we managed to record what he did and how to stop him so others wouldn't be caught off guard again."

That was the book Lintu wanted.

"Memories fade, but Isamea remembered the stories, even if she didn't remember much about her brother." Jan continued.

"But, she's not like that latent guy. Not like Lintu." Christelle knew she was just lost. "We have to get her to understand, that we need to work together. I believe I could convince her, if I could just get some time with her. I mean, I've fought that thing, she must be interested in that."

"Sashine, you need to listen to her. Our daughter can still be helped."

Before Sashine could answer, a chatter started from the deafly silent group around her. Off in the distance, a shadow was moving towards them. She tensed, but Jan smiled and swam toward the shadow.

Not dangerous? What was it?

She definitely wasn't ready for her mother, or Lintu.

Then Finn's familiar shape came into focus, a large round bubble floating on top as Ysians swam next to the whale. Shapes inside the bubble were waving and she finally made out Shirley, Jake, and Pekoi all waving excitedly at Christelle.

Eka Plays With Haze

Eka looked around the Erzincan area. It looked exactly the same as when she'd been there last week, of course without all the drama of Lintu's people finding her and the others. And this time, she was able to portal.

"Yeah. One easy thing." She mumbled to herself.

Memories of last week, in this place, suddenly brought up images of Ke, standing a few feet from her, and gripped her heart and squeezed. Was she really ready to try and get him back here?

Well, what choice did she have? He was her brother.

And this time, you've got to listen.

She dumped Liney's stone fragments out of the bag and on the ground. Sparks seemed to flare momentarily within the deep blue pieces, as if some event was happening deep inside the broken bits. Which seemed to hint to Eka they were still active, just like the one she'd set off.

"That's good. Hopefully enough juice to send out a signal." Eka mumbled to herself.

She moved to push a fragment toward another and, when her fingertip pressed against the jagged edge, something new pulsed through her as the fragment flashed its native blue color. Like a note from a piano resonating inside her, except it was a perfect note, and her body hummed in a warm, familiar way.

But how was it familiar?

She shuddered as her finger came away, staring at the slowing flashes within the fragment as the note faded away. And now she remembered there was a song last time, with the unbroken stone, she'd just been too overwhelmed to realize it was music. And when it was gone, there had been a small emptiness in her.

She pushed a another fragment next to the other, and as they touched a second note joined the first. The song grew as more pieces connected, until her uliee was thrumming with music, a melody of far away places and deep, deep space. Suddenly, a pulse exploded from the puzzle of stone, sending pieces flying and knocking Eka down.

"That was unnecessary." Eka coughed as she brushed off dust and crawled to a kneeling position.

Slowly, a deep blue haze swirled and expanded over the fragments, flashes pulsing with the song still humming inside her. The darkness of space, scattered with star fragments, haunted the haze, like a planetarium laser show playing in the haziness.

"Now that's cool." She whispered in awe then, without a second thought because Eka might have backed away if she'd allowed a second thought, she tentatively reached out to the mist, or opening, or whatever it was, and a planet shot into the scene. She recoiled, falling backwards.

What was that? It almost acted like a game she'd played where new planets zoom into view as you fly closer.

But, it didn't feel like a game.

Her whole being seemed pulled toward the haze and, as she leaned in, the planet grew closer. As the view zoomed to the surface, she could see movement, things hovering above the ground in greenish air. They seemed tiny, wiggling rope-like things. Her hand inched forward and the ground moved under her as her fingers made contact with the haze and the pull grew stronger. Her fingers vibrated and suddenly dissipated, that small bit of her uliee was drawn to the other side of the haze, the bits of light dancing around. She gasped as she seemed to exist on both sides of this haziness.

"What the hell?"

Then she squinted, distracted from her freak out by the scene speeding across the world. She saw small things, which obviously weren't small but far away. And large things. Too large. And were those tentacles? Hovering?

Eka fell back from the vision, her fingers re-solidifying as the haze dissipated.

"It's another world." She whispered to herself as she rubbed the hand now solid hand with her other, the sensation of the song, the travel, lingering with a sense of belonging to something, maybe a home. This is what Liney described, her family traveling through celestial portals, wandering through the universe, to other worlds. All these worlds were their homes just as much as they were family.

Okay. Focus.

"Here for a reason, Eka."

Using the bag to pick up the fragments, she collected the stones, making sure not to touch them, not to get distracted again.

Chills ran along her skin and she spun as a shadowy portal opened not far from the first place she'd seen it. Before anyone could step out, she called Mele out of her and passed the bag to him as she portalled him out to Liney. She wasn't giving Lintu any extra stones.

Now, everything was up to her.

The shadowy darkness completely expanded, the edges as wispy as her own portals, or the one from the stone.

"Hey little bird." Ke smiled slightly at her. "You came back."

The familiar term, the name Sema had always use, threw her focus into a storm momentarily. And in the moment, other portals opened around her. Her skin rippled with warning, jarring her back into the moment. She ran at Ke as He'e and Wallace stepped out of the surrounding haze.

Ke opened his arms, surprise flitting across his face. "Eka, so…"

She opened a portal under him and jumped in after. Ahead of her, Ke tumbled across grass, just as the portal closed behind her. Good thing she'd watched all those open landscapes while she'd traveled, he could be bouncing along asphalt. And this generic, grassy patch near the train tracks should be hard for anyone else to find. Hopefully.

She let Ke tumble to a stop then splay out on the grass, holding his head, before throwing a shield around him. He looked like her brother, a man version, sure, but still Ke. All that growing up, wherever he'd been, she hadn't seen any of it. He hadn't seen her change either. Now, she stood over him, trying to get some semblance of who this person was. Where *her* brother, the person she loved, might be.

His eyes popped open, staring directly into hers. "You can't keep me hidden."

How true was that? "Maybe."

He struggled up, holding his head and stomach. "They can…track me."

She scanned around her. So far, no chills, no portals. She crouched down, touching the clear wall that separated them. "Ke, it's just us."

He gazed up at her, still for a very long moment, before touching his side of the shield, their palms inches away. "I looked for you."

Her breath caught. He'd searched for her, before she even remembered this magical world. When she thought they'd all been dead. If he had found her, she wouldn't be so torn about trusting him. She would have followed him anywhere. But would that have been a good thing? She probably would have walked right into Lintu's service.

Then, an image of him, walking out of a dark portal, flashed through her memory.

Or, he could be lying about looking for me.

Maybe hiding the two of them wasn't completely crazy. She needed time to figure him out and convince him of what really happened.

"You found me." She half-smiled.

He stood, his tall, slender frame brushing the top of the shield. "There's so much…you're so adult."

Eka nodded, quickly smearing a tear off her cheek. "You too." She coughed, clearing her constricted throat.

Ke dropped back down, never taking his eyes away from hers. "Your gifts are amazing."

"Thanks." Was his magic stronger? She hadn't seen him do anything yet, except walk through Lintu's portal. And she could feel it wasn't his magic. "How about yours?" Was he still able to persuade others?

He shrugged. "Can we talk? Without the cage?"

"Not yet." She blurted out. She wasn't sure what he could do. "I'll let you go, after we talk."

Suddenly, a shadow portal opened behind him, Wallace stumbling out at a jerky run toward them. Eka threw a portal under them as she dropped the shield, and they dropped out of the area and onto a field as the portal closed on Wallace's face.

"N…n…ooot aaagaiiin." Ke managed as he bounced across the field, rocking to a rest as Eka sprinted next to him.

"Eka, can you stop, please." Ke rested his head on his hands.

Damnit, they were finding him.

Okay, okay. Spill it before, they show up again.

"I need you to listen. That thing you're with, it's dangerous. It's killing things, people. You have to come with me, stop it." Maybe that wasn't the best presentation she could have made, but she obviously didn't have much time.

Ke's head slowly came up, shaking. "You're wrong. He saved me from her. She killed our parents, almost killed me."

"Ke, that's not how it happened."

"Eka, He'e told me your memories were lost, that that creature changed you. You don't understand any of this. There's so much more than you know."

"Ke, people are dying, because of Lintu. Just like our parents." He had to have seen all that.

"*Not* like our parents." Ke's face contorted, almost unrecognizable. "He's only defended himself. She's corrupted everyone into believing he's dangerous. They're trying to kill him. If you would only listen."

What could she do? She couldn't leave him, but she couldn't lead Wallace and He'e to any Wakers. How could she hide him until she could make him understand.

Chills grabbed her attention, and she started a portal.

"We'll kill all the Wakers on that ship if you go." Wallace's stilted voice stopped her. He'd already found them and it hadn't even been five minutes. She was running out of options. Or was out.

She glanced at Wallace, then back at Ke. "How can you believe him, when they'd kill all those people."

"Eka, no one will get hurt, if you come with us. I promise. He just needs your help." Ke's face had lost its edge. "You'll see he just wants help."

Wallace stood, staring. "I'll give the signal if you disappear again."

Signal who? Could Lintu do that to an entire ship? Could He'e? Or were there more? Maybe the Nalo?

She glanced between the two, the images of Jason, Quinn, Brigg, and all the others on the ship unaware of any danger, made up her mind. She couldn't reach them, and even if she did, they were defenseless. She had to protect them. But, she could let Liney know what was going on. Maybe she could even figure out what Lintu's next move would be.

"Fine." She released Ke. He moved toward her, but stopped when she stepped back. He sagged for a moment, then straightened and moved ahead of Wallace to the portal. "You'll have to follow this way."

Eka shuddered, sensations of the cold emptiness from that night on the island in Manatee Isles, where she'd first encountered Lintu and what he could do, swept through her. This really sucked. She breathed deeply in and slowly followed, Wallace marching jerkily behind her. The first touch of dark gray haze hit her just like she remembered it, goosebumps erupting from her skin as she stepped back into Wallace.

She spun. "Hey. Some room."

Wallace, empty eyes, just stared, but didn't push. "Don't have all day." His voice didn't even sound like his. Eka examined his awkward limbs, resting in ways that still conjured images of marionettes.

Ugh! This will not happen to me.

She turned back to the portal and took her first step through. But, right before she passed into the haze, an image of her with Ke and Wallace, headed to Lintu, left her and went searching for Mele.

Christelle Finds A Crystal

A small pebble floated up in front of Christelle and Tine. The Ysian girl slumped, which was an amazing posture as she was literally floating in water, her newly upgraded energy was flagging. Christelle slipped her hand under the pebble. "Hey." She took Tine's hand and lowered the pebble into it. "You can do this."

"But, I need something bigger. The energy is too small in that…," the girl seemed ready to fling the small stone, "that tiny rock!"

Christelle snatched it back. "Look, you don't need a huge boulder to raise the energy." Christelle opened her palm, the tiny bit of rock, a piece of Gaia, old and weathered. She closed her eyes, sensing warmth, calm, the planet inside the tiny rock, singing its own song. Her uliee flowed into it, moving and spiraling until it entrained to the melody. Christelle's uliee rose up, amplifying the song and pulling the stone's energy with it until it exploded out of the stone and toward the fire, which was the next piece in this new version of the device she was working on. But the stone's energy didn't entwine with fire energy, as Klian wasn't ready. So much for preparations. But a series of gasps escaped from the members of Tine's team, grabbing all their attentions.

Christelle smiled a bit. She hadn't taught in a while, but still enjoyed the breakthroughs.

Tine studied the stone and her own uliee.

Christelle glanced at the group. She'd upgraded each one of them so easily, unlike the others back in Ys. She'd almost forgotten how easily Wakers could connect to the world. "This device, or entity, really…"

"Wait, entity? I thought it was just a device you constructed." Tine asked.

Christelle smiled at the girl. "We're using it as a device to channel Gaian energy. And when Sema and Win," her stomach tightened at the thought of Sema and she sighed, "built their version of the device, they created a container whose purpose was just to hold all the pieces. They thought the important parts of the device were the pieces and the energy they contained and to get these parts active, they just needed a burst of intense energy to jump start it. I think they believed that the Gaian energy of each piece would activate the energy of the next and then the pieces would work together, like trying to push something and adding more people to help push it. When all of these pieces, representing all of the different parts of Gaian energy, were activated in the right order so they could activate the next piece, and when they were all pushing together, the device would be able to send out a huge wave of energy, the size of the wave based on how much each piece was pushing."

Tine's eyes were glazing over.

Do I suck at teaching now?

"Hey." She tapped Tine's hand and the girl blinked her focus back. "Sorry for that info overload. Just know that they probably saw it all wrong, even though it worked. I believe this whole thing is alive. Alive!" Christelle through her hands in the air.

Tine just stared, along with the rest of the kids in their configuration. At least her eyes weren't glazed over anymore.

Christelle dropped her arms. "Sorry, Asleep thing. Anyway, it's alive, just like everything around us."

And we're part of this device's life, somehow.

And she wasn't sure how to explain that, so instead, she held out the stone as she pointed to the representatives of all Gaia's gifts, held by more than a dozen Ysians forming the circle. Like the piece of coral held by a boy across from her, or the piece of seaweed held in the young woman's hand on his right, and fire, somehow burning *in* water now, miraculously, hovering over the hand of the young man, Klian, next to her.

She still grinned at the reality of underwater fire.

So cool.

"You are Wakers…"

"Ysians!" Klian protested.

"And Wakers." She raised her eyebrows and Klian quieted. "Which means your spirit is in tune with Gaia. As you each hold a piece of Gaia, you are, together, the contain and when your Gaian spirit vibrates with the energy of the piece you hold, it's like, I don't know, playing an instrument."

"What's an instrument?" Klian, interrupted and they all murmured a similar question.

"Um…" How did she explain it. These people had been underwater their whole lives. "Um, you know when whales make those long calls?"

They all nodded.

"That's like a song. Using a voice to create beautiful sounds."

"Beautiful?" Klisn questioned.

"It's beautiful, soulful." Tine glared at him.

"Maybe annoying." He shook his head. "Like you."

"Okay." Christelle held up her hand. "Music is a matter of taste, but Asleep have instruments made out of things, like wood, that make sounds like that. And when you put many instruments together, like lots of whales making these sounds, the total sound can be incredible, more than any individual instrument can make." She gave them a minute to process this.

"And that's what I believe happens here. Your Gaian uliee and spirit vibrates with the energy of the material you're holding and creates a new energy, different than yours or the material's, something that emerged from the two." There were gasps around the group.

"This isn't just a weapon we're building to stop Lintu." She continued. "Right now, each of you can access more of Gaia than any regular Waker or Ysian. But you're just one person, and it's not enough." Shivers ran through her at flashes of her trying to transmit her uliee through the small, static device Sema and Win had made and into Lintu. At the partial failure and aftermath. If this worked, these people, her people, wouldn't have to watch Lintu hurt others or escape. They wouldn't have to wonder where he might turn up next or who he might kill. "This is a connection to your gifts, to your community, to the Waker world and Gaia. So, you're uliee has to sing to the part of Gaia in your hand." A few snickers, and a few 'sing to this', rippled through the group and Christelle tried not to smile at the lightheartedness. Overly seriousness was something she'd needed to cleanse from herself, leftover bits of the old Chriselle still lingering.

"Hey!" Tine scowled at the group. "Listen! No messing around."

But sometimes a leader needed to be serious, balance was really the key. Christelle nodded at Tine, her serious view of leadership seemingly overwhelming her. "She's right." The group grew quiet. "Each of you need to hear Gaia's song in the piece of her you hold, to merge with the part that part of her, then let that each of the new uliee merge collectively, to create the power needed to stop Lintu. You're strong enough, connected enough, to do this. Just let go and let the gift guide you." A surge of energy ran through Christelle as the kids really leaned in. "You're a team and with the right timing, I believe you'll create a new spiritual uliee and the whole thing will come alive at that moment. And when that happens, the spiritual uliee of this…being will have so much energy kick Lintu's a…"

Tine coughed at that moment, catching Christelle at the best moment of her speech.

As she took a breath, Christelle noticed that every Ysian was studying the small piece of the device they held. The group whispered to each other while examining the embodiment of their gifts. Some were shaking their heads, others sagged, their energy, after so much practice, as low as Tine's but also maybe overwhelmed with what all this meant.

"Break time." Christelle announced and a sense of relief swept the group.

"But, we need more practice." Tine watched the scattering group, probably ready to chase them down and drag them back.

"Hey." Christelle stepped in front of her and laid her hand on Tine's shoulder. "Everyone needs rest, including you."

"But, what if we're attacked right now? We're not ready."

"And you won't be any good exhausted. Just rest a bit, okay. You can round everyone up soon."

Tine huffed, but nodded. "Fine."

Christelle watched her swim off. Were they ready? This new configuration was so much more powerful, but was it enough?

I don't know.

A soft touch on her shoulder and she whirled around.

"Don't know what?" Pekoi asked, smiling down at her as he pulled his hand back inside his bubble. She still thought the bubbles were a cool Ysian trick to let non-Ysians into their world.

Behind them, Finn's tail disappeared.

"How you always sneak up on me, I just don't know." She frowned, sliding into the bubble with him. She still hadn't cracked his stealthiness.

"Got to keep the mystery up, keep you guessing." He leaned in close. "Interested."

A shiver went down her spine, her favorite kind of shiver. "I think I have an overload of mysteries right now."

He raised his eyebrows briefly. "Not my kind of mystery." Then he leaned in and she lost her whole train of thought. It just derailed, lit on fire, then exploded.

She lay next to Pekoi in their coral hut, his familiar snoring filling a hole she didn't know was there. She snuggled in closer, his heartbeat lightly tapping her ear. When had she gotten used to this? To him? To this world and her life?

If she took out all the extra-worldly, and family, drama, this new life was almost perfect.

She studied his face, the contours as familiar as his snoring, then she brushed his cheek.

"Can't sleep." Pekoi's eyebrow's waggled as his eyes opened and he turned toward her, readjusting their bodies.

"Too distracted." Her hand wandered until he caught his breath and his lips quickly found hers.

"Christelle!" Shirley's voice raced through the door and right in between them.

They both sighed as Christelle rolled out of the bed and trudged to the door. "Hey Grams." She cracked the door and peaked through.

"Hey kiddo, we'd like to chat with you."

"We?"

"Sashine's here too."

Christelle looked back at Pekoi. 'Both' he mouthed and shook his head at some imagined problem she'd caused.

"Just give me a moment."

"Tell that boy you'll be back later."

Christelle's face flamed hot and she slammed the door then ran to pick up her clothes. Pekoi grabbed her hand as she dressed, trying to pull her back toward him. "They can wait a moment."

She pulled her hand out of his, reluctantly, and kept dressing. "They're right outside the door."

"They can't hear anything." He half-heartedly dove for her, all his assets in full view.

Out of his reach, she threw the sheet over him. "I'll be back." As she turned, his hand shot out from the sheet and pulled her on top of his quickly rolled over body. She loved his body.

"Don't take too long." He breathed, their lips touching and all she could do is nod.

She did manage to crawl off him and make it to the door, refusing her body a backward glance. With a sigh, she finally squeezed out the crack she'd left between door and hut and slid out of the bubble around the rock hut, almost tumbling into Sashine. Going from air-breathing in the hut that Pekoi stayed in, to water-breathing in the surrounding ocean, wasn't as tricky as it first was, but it always took her breath away for a moment. Breathing deeply, she caught her grandmother in a hug as Sashine stopped her momentum.

"Christelle." Sashine hugged her back. "So happy to see you too."

Christelle giggled, her face against Sashine's shoulder. "So," she stepped back. "What are you doing here?"

"We're here to chat about the device."

They dragged her out for this?

"There's a lot of interest up top." Christelle spun to find Shirley floating behind her. "I'd love to give you kids a lifetime in that hut, but things are getting crazier."

"What happened?"

Sashine took Christelle's arm, gliding her past Shirley's bubble as they swam away from the hut.

"Always loved these bubble things." Shirley did a backward flip, the gravity seemed almost half inside them. "Woot!"

A ghost of a smile flitted across Sashine's face. "Shirley, focus."

They stopped at a small area where children usually hung out after school. Well, at least Christelle believed they were in some sort of school, although she had no idea what they learned. Maybe someday she'd discover that and all the other mundane parts of Ysian lives. Or Waker lives for that matter.

"There've been more attacks." Sashine sighed.

"That's why we came lookin' for you." Shirley sat cross-legged, floating in the bubble. "Good thing you'd left Ys or we would've ended up there."

Christelle nodded. "Guess you heard about our escape."

"Everyone's heard!" Shirley whistled, grinning. "You've got yourself a reputation. That extra-terrestrial demon better watch out. My granddaughter's gonna kick its…"

"We need to know how the device is going." Sashine briefly eyed Shirley. "We feel like the, um, 'extraterrestrial demon' is getting closer to whatever its plan is."

"Um yeah. I think we have it, they just need more practice."

Sashine rubbed a green-blue stone hanging from her neck. "I hope it's enough."

"Me too." Christelle blinked as the stone flared with tiny bright spots that left light spots behind her eyelids. She rubbed her eyes, trying to erase them. "What's that?"

Sashine lifted the stone, turning it over. "It's one of the crystals I talked about. Gaia made it for me, when I became Keeper. It's tuned to the ocean, amplifies my connection to it." The left corner of her mouth quirked up and she lowered her voice. "Helps me talk with the ocean, when I need someone to help me with your grandfather." She waggled her eyebrows.

"Okay, maybe I don't…wait, talk with the ocean?"

Sashine frowned. "Yessss? Certain Ysians can talk with the spirits."

Unlike the other Wakers she'd met, including Ysians, Sashine seemed completely at ease with spirits. Did that mean she'd always known about them? Had worked with them. The crystal flashed again and thoughts of spirits turned to the crystal. Christelle touched it and the vibrations of the song shook through her. "Whoa." She dropped her hand. "Do you still have those other crystals?"

Sashine nodded slowly, her frown deepening.

"What'cha thinking kiddo?" Shirley looked between Christelle and the crystal.

"Do you know how to store energy in them?"

Sashine nodded, even more slowly.

"Then I think I might have the key to this entity device thingy."

"The what?" Both her grandmothers seemed to sing the question together.

Maybe she needed to name the device, or entity, to help people get what she was talking about. "I'll explain on the way. Right now, we need the crystals." Hope blossomed in her for the first time in a while.

"That's just what I was hoping to hear." Christelle froze at the voice, only turning after Sashine's eyes grew large at the figure behind her. Shirley's face didn't give away much, as usual.

"Mom." Christelle slowly turned to find Isamea and her Ysian contingent hovering close by.

Eka Sees The Lighter

Eka shivered as she stepped out of the shadowy portal, trying to shake off the oily bits it left covering her. Her own portal was not only part of her, but connected her to the energy around her, resonating with her and the world. Energy that sang of planets, and space, and life.

This trip was like submitting her soul to a vacuum cleaner, it grabbed at her energy and tried pulling, somehow unable to remove it from her.

Ahead, Ke stood on a rocky outcrop waiting for her, but instead of heading right to him, she spun completely around. Below, a beach spread out, moonlight reflecting in a lazy, wavering line from the shore to the distant horizon. She squinted. Somehow, the moonlight didn't seem to shine as brightly closer to shore. All around her, the normal flow of energy was gone, only bits of energy sparked anywhere. Trees, rocks, shrubs, flowers, all almost dead, so much like Dark Cove, back in Manatee Isles after Lintu destroyed it. That's what he did with everything he touched, destroyed it.

She glanced over at Ke. How did he not see that?

He was all alone, scared. He'd just seen Mom and Dad die, thought Lintu had saved him. He was just a kid that lived his whole life with a murderer and kidnapper. No one was there to save him.

That had to be it. But she was here now, she'd save him.

"Come on." Ke motioned, his brows furrowed. "This way."

She took a deep breath and stepped toward him, wishing they were anywhere else.

They trudged up the rocks, up the side of a worn away volcano, fewer and fewer bits of energy around them. It reminded her of how the world looked before she was re-initiated into the Waker world. Off to her side, a large pile of ash sat amongst the dead trees, energy completely missing. She refused to ponder what that pile used to be but her heart raced and her legs tried to turn around. Somehow, she managed to stop them.

I can always portal out if things get bad. And this may be the only way to really find out what's happening. This could help the others. And talk with Ke.

A deep breath later, she trudged up again, stopping behind Ke on a ledge that emptied into a dark hole in the cliff.

Of course. A deep, dark cave. What could go wrong?

Ke smiled briefly then disappeared into the blackness. Was she really going to follow him into that?

Apparently she was because her foot stepped right into the pitch black and dragged her whole body with it. All around her, darkness engulfed her, slowing her to a stop. "Ke?"

There was silence for forever. Should she turn back? Feel her way forward? Then, she jumped as Ke's hand slid into hers and pulled her around a corner. Dull lights flickered against the dead stone, the light barely reaching past the light fixtures.

Did they have electricity here? She stumbled after Ke, the lack of life energy disorienting. His hand seemed cold against hers and almost slippery. Oily.

She jerked her hand back, rubbing it as he glanced at her. "What?"

Eka shook her head. "Nothing." She was probably just creeped out by all the missing energy.

Ke shrugged and continued along a slightly lit path and Eka continued to follow, winding down into the island. The dull lights flickered against non-descript dead walls, disorienting her. Would she even be able to jump back here if she needed to come back? This place didn't have a 'feel' to it.

Would she even *want* to jump back here?

"Wait in here." Ke pointed toward a door, the room beyond barely lit.

"Why?"

"I've got to do some things before they're ready for you. And He's not back yet."

Eka stuck her head in the little cave. "You're just dumping me? How long am I gonna sit here?" This was not what she expected. How was she gonna reach him if he takes off.

"Just stay here, okay? I'll be back later."

She studied Ke. "Will you promise to talk with me?"

Ke looked down the hall then back at her. He seemed to really look at her for a moment. "Sure. I just need to go for now."

Eka finally nodded and stepped in the room as Ke left. She paced around the dimly lit, sterile room. This whole place just didn't make sense. There was nothing here. What were they doing? Did they really need a base, if it's just a bunch of lights in some rooms?

She turned at the far wall of the tiny space and paused, staring at her hands. A faint shimmer went through her uliee, nudging her back toward the door.

Weird.

Had it done this before? She couldn't remember, but she'd only been in a place this dead once. And she hadn't been doing much thinking.

The rocky hallways seemed empty, and Ke was gone for who knows how long, so she quietly left the room, following some faint pull. She tried to move stealthily, but even her lightest steps seemed to echo in these hallways, the emptiness bouncing the sound around her like a pinball.

How long she walked, she wasn't sure but the tug grew stronger until she stopped in front of a wall of dark energy. Her uliee might as well be a large neon arrow pointing behind the darkness.

"I really don't want to go through that."

If her uliee could slap her, her cheeks would be glowing.

"Fine. I'll go. But I'm going to need a week in a tub to get all this crappy energy off me." She inhaled and stuck her hand through, her body tensing at the sliminess. Other than the hungry, pulling sensation, nothing happened. So, she slid through into another poorly lit room.

Weak gasps escaped a number of Wakers scattered around the space, laying prone or propped against the wall. The ones closest to her shuffled quickly away.

"Uh. Hey?" Eka half smiled at them.

One of the Wakers slowly rose, using the wall as support. "Who are you?" She croaked.

"Eka." Who were these people? Why were they here?

"Eka?" A young man with brown hair coughed as he squinted at her. "It's Pim."

"Pim?" She crossed to him as others scooted away, and squatted down. Rings shadowed his eyes and his skin seemed pale and yellow. But she remembered his face, a lighter from Hapton's. "What happened to you?

"I was traveling down through Mexico when something attacked my uliee. Next thing I knew, I was here. What are you doing here? Did they grab you too?"

She shook her head.

His eyes grew large and he shrunk back. "Are you with them?"

She shook her head again.

"Then what are you doing here?" The only standing Waker asked.

She took in all the Wakers, their weakness, exhaustion. Were all of them prisoners? Did it matter? "I'm trying to find out what they're doing."

"You *snuck* in here?" Pim whispered.

"I…followed someone. Do you know why they brought you here?" Eka asked, hoping her answer was enough.

"They need lighters." Pim shuddered, his voice cracking. "For some stone."

"Wait, a dark blue stone, with flares of light?"

Pim nodded.

Leana's story zipped back into her mind.

"How do you know about the stone?" The standing woman butted in again. She seemed to be the leader or spokesperson of the group.

"I've…touched it." Eka glanced up at the woman then back at Pim, making sure they both heard. "Have you touched it?

Pim nodded and shuddered again.

"Did you feel anything?"

"Like what?" His voice seemed so small.

"I don't know. Like space, or planets, or something." Okay, that sounded really weird when she said it out loud.

"Yeah." A nearby man said. "At least I think so. I thought I heard a humming…"

"Like a song?" Eka stared at him.

He shrugged. "Maybe."

She examined Pim, really looking at his uliee. Weak, Gaian uliee flowed in him, but every now and then she caught a glimpse of something else. Something deep blue, like her uliee. She hadn't seen many lighters, they'd always been such loners, but Eric, on the ship, had energy like this.

Maybe their uliee wasn't all Gaian. Like hers. But why? There'd been lighters long before Irida. So where'd it come from? Were there other celestials that came here? Who would know?

"Look." The vocal woman walked over. "You slipped in here, have touched that stone, are free to roam, and you're asking us questions. Your uliee isn't Waker uliee. Who are you? What's going on?"

She couldn't leave them here to be used for Lintu's plan, but what if there were more? "Are there any more of you?"

The woman crossed her arms. "You need to answer for a change."

Eka took a deep breath and grabbed the woman's hand.

Hope I'm right about their energy and this works like it did when Christelle upgraded other Wakers.

Uliee flowed out of Eka and into the woman, finding a small strand of non-Gaian energy and connecting. The woman's scowl morphed into seeming surprise and the gray faded from her dark brown hue. Eka dropped her hand as she stared at it.

"Woot woot! I was right!" Eka did a small dance before noticing the others were just staring.

"What? How?" The woman just sputtered.

"Look, I can help, but I need to know if there are any other prisoners here."

The woman shook her head, still staring at her hands. "I don't know." Around the room, that seemed to be the consensus.

"Okay, I have to check, but I'll be back." Before anyone could respond, she slipped back out through the dark barrier and leaned against a cold, dead wall.

What was she doing? She wasn't a hero, she was here for information and to save Ke.

"I can't just leave them." But if she took them out, her chances of time with Ke were small. "One step at a time. See if there's anyone else."

She closed her eyes and relaxed, trying to sense anything that might lead her to where others were. After a long moment, her energy shimmered again, this time even fainter. She stood for a long while, trying to figure out the path. Finally, she headed downward.

The dead space and flickering lights grated against her spirit after walking for what seemed like years. "Couldn't they at least hang a picture or something." She stopped for the hundredth time, trying to orient to her uliee again and almost missed the small opening by her feet. Her energy had stopped pulling.

"Yeah, something's here." She dropped to her knees and examined the short tunnel that glowed dimly at the other end. "Okay, just through a short, tiny tunnel, in a dead island, to a dimly lit room. It'll be great." Eka slowly started in, crossing the echoey floor, and finally emerging onto a wide ledge encircling a large cavern, a few closed doors around the edges.

"Had to find a hole, not a door. Awesome." Her eyes almost rolled back in her head.

Voices erupted from below the lip of the ledge and Eka crawled to the edge to peer over the side. She clamped her hand over her mouth as her brain worked to not understand the scene below.

A group that seemed to be Nalos, now with gray, oily energy running through them, stood in the middle of the cavern. Ringed around them were bodies. Animals that must have lived on the island, lay decaying near the cave walls. Scattered amongst them were human bodies, probably Wakers. But why hadn't their bodies disappeared? Had their deaths affected that?

Then a Nalo started dragging someone toward the middle of the room. A waker. He stumbled, uliee almost gone, and fell at the groups' feet.

"Try now." A large Nalo man pushed a small wiry Nalo woman close to the fallen Waker. "Prove you deserve this, others would love to have what's left."

The small woman scowled and pulled up the man's face by his hair.

"Please, no." He barely whispered.

"Shut up." She spat back and slapped her palm on his exposed chest. Gaian uliee, faint in him, ripped away from his body so violently he convulsed. And unlike the others, his body started to break apart, disintegrate, his wide eyes disappearing into nothing.

"Finally got it right." The giant of a man slapped her back.

"Damn right." She licked her lips and kicked the pile. "Always hated him."

"Eka."

She spun at her name, Ke standing over her. Tears stung her cheeks and her brain still wouldn't work.

"You shouldn't be here."

"Ke. You have to stop all this. Please."

"Eka, it'll be alright. You've just got to see the big picture."

No. No. No.

She shook her head, wrenching her own neck. "Ke, you don't know what you're saying. That thing took you, kept you as its prisoner. You have to see, this is wrong."

"You're the one that doesn't get it. How can you defend those cowards that took your memories? Thought you were less? Oh, I know all about that. He'e told me how they'd stolen your memories, abandoned me, how it was her that tried to find me and protect you. And how they turned you against her, against Lintu."

How many stories had He'e fed him?

"Ke, you have no idea."

And he was suddenly glaring at her. "No! You don't understand. All those Wakers, thinking they deserved their powers, that they were better! Well, look at them now!" He pointed down to the Nalos, to the bodies. "They thought we didn't matter, that we were lower than them. That we were as worthless as the Asleep." He leaned toward her. "Guess who has the power now." He whispered, but somehow it shook her worse than any yell. "And it's all because of Him. He made us strong, stronger than them. And they'll all pay." Then he straightened up, dropping the anger as a smile spread.

All Eka could do was stare up at him.

"With your powers, we can open that door, his friends can come through, change this world forever. He'll be ready at the new moon. And we don't need those useless lighters anymore."

He knew. All along, he knew.

How did I not see…I…

He looked down at the Nalos again. "We have some new ones available, so get anyone that needs a boast ready."

No!

Eka stared up at Ke one last time, all traces of her brother gone. "I loved you." She finally whispered and portaled away, Ke's eyes growing large as he disappeared from her view.

She tumbled into the lighters' prison, everyone scrambling away. "We have to go now!"

"What are you talking about?"

A tingling started under her skin. They were portaling to her. She ran to each lighter, and each one disappeared as she touched them. They tried to move away, but were too weak to really fight. Finally a break.

When she got to Pim, the last, Ke was running out of a dark, hazy portal, right at them. She dove at Pim and they both portaled as Ke's hand glanced off her foot. She rolled with Pim on the deck of the ship, slamming into a tree in a tangle of limbs. Around her, lighters were struggling up. Eka jumped up as Mele flew at her. "Go get Jason." She spun to the lighters.

"How did you get us here?"

"Where are we?"

Eka whistled, startling into silence the disoriented crowd.

"Eka, what's going on?" Jason, at first blurry-eyed, looked at the lighters as woke up immediately. "Who are these people?"

"Jason, I don't have time to discuss. Is there anywhere safe the ship can go? Hurry."

"I, uh, I'll get the captain." He ran off.

"Mele, go find Christelle." The little specter flew off again, chattering to her as it disappeared.

Eka ran to the edge of the ship, and imagined a shield covering the entire hull. Her energy rolled out of her, slowly engulfing the ship in a transparent shield.

Gasps came from behind her, probably the lighters. Who else would be up at this hour.

She laughed through the strain, thinking how Wakers kept the schedule of teenagers. Or Vampires. "Maybe that's where all those stories came from." Who knew?

Halfway through the shielding, her energy strained and the shield started to grow thin. "Really? Now?"

Then the woman she'd dumped energy into was there next to her, her uliee flowing into Eka's and the shielding started again. More lighters joined, small energy magnifying as the group grew, until they finally had the ship in a bubble.

"What are you doing!" The captain ran at them.

"You need to hide." Eka grimaced at the captain. "There might be an attack heading here."

After studying the group and shield for a moment, he nodded and left.

Mele suddenly appeared again, chattering something about Christelle and danger. "Damnit." She looked at the shield, stable now, then the lighters. "I need you to keep this up. It'll protect you from them."

The woman nodded.

Eka turned back to Mele and portaled after her, hoping Christelle was just having a bad day.

Christelle Pops A Bubble

"Hello Christelle. Seems you left in a hurry." Isamea turned to Sashine. "Hello. Seems we finally caught up with you."

"Isamea. You aren't welcome here."

"You don't get to make decisions for anyone any more."

Christelle floated between the two, blocking their increasingly erratic energy. "We should all talk."

"Nothing to say." Isamea and Sashine's voices spoke in unison, somehow of the same mind at that moment.

"Mom, please. We can talk. We all want the same thing. To stop Lintu." Christelle's voice cracked as she tried to find her mother in the form in front of her.

"Christelle." Isamea paused, looking at her daughter for a long moment. "I…I missed you."

"I missed you too." Unexpected tears rolled down Christelle's face, which was a weird sensation underwater. "So much." She stepped into her mother's arms and she was lost in the deep hug.

"I dreamed about seeing you again, every day." Isamea whispered as she sank into Christelle.

Christelle's body seemed to sag so deeply it lost form. Her mother was holding her. Holding her. "Me too." Short sentences was all she managed.

"It hurt so much to leave you."

"I…thought you were dead." Christelle cried. Until Isamea's body tightened.

"They killed me." Isamea's arms slowly dropped from Christelle. "Killed our family."

"Mom?" Christelle hiccuped and looked up, into growing rage, and stepped back. "You're not dead, you're here."

Isamea narrowed her eyes and looked up at the others. "All this time, neither one of you made it right. My daughter and my family was gone and our world was no safer. You failed. All of you. Now, I'll make it right, make our world right."

"Isamea." Jake suddenly floated next to Shirley. "Our family is here. Now. You don't have to leave again. Our daughter, she's back."

Isamea's anger disappeared briefly as she saw Jake, then flared back. "No! They were wrong, and they destroyed us. But I can make this right and the world will be safe for us." She glared at Shirley and Sashine. "And from them. And my daughter can help make the world a place where no one will have to go through what we did. Because she knows how to make the device work." Isamea looked at Christelle. "We can defeat that thing, Lintu, reorder the Ysian and Waker worlds."

She wants to…rule everyone? Christelle shook her head and stepped backwards. "It's not a weapon to use against Wakers."

Isamea opened her hands. "No one need force us to use it. Wakers will see how lost they are, hiding from the Asleep, following orders from a dead spirit. And Ysians will stand where they belong, as the strongest, the leaders."

She really wants to control everyone. Christelle stepped back, until she bumped into Jake, who wrapped his arms around her. "I can't do that."

From behind Isamea, strange, Asleep type machines glided up, halting a bit away. They reminded Christelle of a cross between a submarine and a tank, but with dark sludge-like energy flowing across them. Her stomach clenched. She knew what that energy did. Steal the life out of others.

"You're stealing energy?" Christelle starred directly at her mother.

Isamea looked back at the machines. "I didn't say bring them up." She growled at Nor then turned back to her daughter. "No one has been hurt. We just took a little, stored it in those crystals. You've got to understand, we needed the energy, to power these machines. They'll help us defeat Lintu but, we need that device to make sure we win, especially now that Ysians gifts are…troubled. And with your help, maybe we can get our gifts back and use all these tools to not only defeat that thing, but lead the world. If you could just give us the device, show us how to work it, help us."

The Ysians, Isamea's Ysians, were definitely troubled. They'd lost their connection to Gaia and her energy, to all energy. Christelle shook her head, her hopes of reconnecting with her mother sinking. Her mother was out of control. Around Christelle, strong uliee sparked inside tense, outcast Ysians.

And across from her, the dark energy pulsed.

"We all need the device." Christelle stood against her mom. Against. How could she fight her, her own mother?

Before she could even voice her sorrow to Isamea, a shadowy pulse erupted from one of the machines behind Isamea. The dark energy twisted as it hurled toward Christelle, a whirlwind of water pulling at the energy around it and leaving a hollow path of liquid behind it.

Before Christelle could attempt a defense, Jake threw her to the side and the pulse slammed into him, exploding his protective bubble and wrapping him in a dark, energy-chewing sludge. Christelle scrabbled up, trying to blast the energy off him or create another bubble, but it only ate any uliee she used. Somewhere, she heard a muted scream and glanced up to see Sashine and Jan dragging Shirley to safety, expressions of bewilderment to disbelief across their faces. She only hoped Pekoi was still in the hut because she couldn't even begin to help anyone else as she dumped uliee into her father.

"No!" Isamea tore into the energy, trying to get to him, but her attempts were more useless than Christelle's.

Explosive sounds around her tried to grab Christelle's attention but all she could do was hold her father, his energy draining, air leaving. She tried to breath for him but he wasn't taking her air. She dragged his body toward the hut he had, dark bits of sludge hitting the ground around her and on on her face and hands, faint stings as she made it inside the bubble hut and dropped Jake.

"Dad." She shook him, eyes closed, water dribbling out of his mouth. "Dad!" She tried the CPR she remembered from that one class she'd gone to at some community center, but he just lay there, his body shaking from her compressions. Air went in, lungs compressed, but he wasn't waking, just staring. That's when she realized, the darkness was gone. The bubble, supported with energy, held. Because the leach energy was gone. There was nothing left in him to take.

"Jake?"

Christelle spun to face Isamea hovering in the doorway. "You!" She spat out, sending a whirlwind through the room, hitting Isamea and blowing her out of the bubble, exploding it. Christelle stepped into the rushing water as if it didn't exist and strode toward Isamea. "You killed him."

Isamea crawled back, her eyes darting to Jake then Christelle. "Christelle, I didn't…this wasn't supposed to happen." She turned to where her machines had been and opened her mouth, then froze. Christelle, uliee exploding in her, blinked as something flew past her, and she looked up to find a battlefield of dark energy and fighting Ysians. All around her pulses of shadows drained energy and uliee, the Gaian energy unable to stop the onslaught. And there wasn't enough time, or exiled Ysians, to get the entity together. They needed to retreat, but where would they go?

A contingent of military Ysians ran up, surrounding Isamea, holding…guns? Guns with the same dark energy as the machines. They aimed at Christelle.

"No!" Isamea shouted as Christelle swept away the ground under them and they dropped, giving her time to swim away.

Water suddenly churned next to Christelle, spitting out Eka whose eyes grew large as she floundered in the water. Christelle formed a bubble around them quickly.

"What the hell is going on?" Eka glanced around, grabbing Christelle and ducking as dark energy skimmed over their enclosure.

"Talk later. Can you get everyone not using weapons out?"

Eka nodded and disappeared. Apparently she didn't even need a portal anymore.

All around her, Ysians, her Ysians, started disappearing. Christelle swam back to Jake just as Eka made it to her and jumped her out of there. The last thing Christelle saw was her mother staring blankly at her and Jakes' disappearing forms.

Christelle Hates The Plan

Christelle stared at Eka, the barn, and the ship hovering over it. A numbness threatened to overtake her and she grabbed onto any thought that wasn't about her father. "This is where you stayed?"

Eka opened her mouth to say something then, apparently changed her mind and closed it. She scanned the area instead and shrugged. "Kinda felt out in the middle of nowhere so a little safer."

Christelle barely heard Eka's answer as she fought back a potential torrent of tears. Shaking her head to clear it, she finally took in the vast fields around them. "Okay. I can see that. But isn't there an owner?" She asked, trying to distract herself.

Eka sighed, then shrugged again. "No one ever showed up."

At that moment, the barn shuddered in the wind and leaned just a bit more toward toppling.

Christelle raised her brows and finally saw the barn without the distraction of her internal chaos. They both cocked their heads slightly, toward the tilt. "That's…comforting." Just then, Pekoi touched down next to her, Fluffy wrapped around his head and neck, his hair swirling in the Fluffy breeze. Was that even comfortable?

Christelle shook her head clear as he leaned in for a kiss, his smile not relieving her heart like it usually did. Her father's body gone, in the way all Wakers' bodies disappeared after death, so she hadn't had an opportunity to bury him. Not only that, but they'd all just barely made it here on the ship, so there hadn't even been time for personal grief. And traveling in daylight, trying to hide in plain sight from Lintu, military Ysians, and any Asleep, had pushed her and everyone else to their limits. Now, hidden in the shadows of night and countryside, most of them were passed out, catching up on too little sleep.

Everyone but a few.

"Does the device-thing work?" Eka blurted out.

Christelle's heart dropped, images of her father's energy fading. Right now, there was nothing to protect him or any of the others from Lintu. Or her mom. "I don't know." She almost spat.

"Christelle?" Eka reached out but Pekoi shook his head from next to Christelle.

"We didn't get a chance to test it before the attack." Pekoi sighed.

"Damn." Eka's whole body sagged.

"We can still get it together." Christelle let out a deep breath. She finally understood Eka's need to push off thoughts of Sema's death. Christelle couldn't afford to break down right now, too many people depended on her. She had to be focused for now and later she could mourn her dad.

In fact, they needed to be ready yesterday. Not tomorrow. "In theory, it works. So we'll have to try it right away." Before anything else happens.

They were all thinking it.

A wind blew across them, then out over the field. Grass tops, glowing with faint green energy, undulated under the silver energy of the passing wind. Everything seemed so normal here, in this moment. Could she hold on to it a little longer?

"Lintu and…others were keeping Wakers prisoner. Lighters, just like Leana describe." Eka's arms folded across her chest, as if a chill held her, and her gaze followed the wind as well. "I think they have others, I just didn't have time to find them." Eka's voice almost broke and Christelle briefly squeezed her arm.

All the lighters Eka had freed were trying to recover with the healers but Christelle wasn't sure they'd all survive. How were they even going to fight Lintu, or his people, with what they had right now? She glanced at Eka. What about her brother, who she wouldn't talk about. How the hell were they supposed to go up against him if Eka wasn't willing to fight him? Would she protect him?

"I think I could find any other lighters Lintu has, if I go back." Eka's voice broke her thoughts.

"What? No." Christelle couldn't let her disappear into that uncertainty.

Eka might be capable of handling magic attacks but she seemed no where near ready to deal with Ke. "Besides, they'll be expecting you to portal in, looking for your uliee. How will you get in without them noticing?"

Eka smiled at her. "I've got this." Her smile dropped as her eyes seemed to focus on something internal. "I can't let them open that rift again. I can't let more like Lintu through."

"You have no plan." The words were out before Christelle realized what she'd said.

"As if we ever have a plan." Eka's smile was back, but Christelle recognized the bravado.

"Eka, this isn't like every other time. There are enemies everywhere and you'll be alone."

Pekoi, silently watching them, put his hand on Christelle's arm and she sighed. Eka wasn't going to change her mind. And honestly, she'd probably do the same in those circumstances.

"Just be careful. Okay?" This stupid statement was all she had to give Eka at that moment and it wasn't nearly enough for the best friend she'd ever had.

Eka smiled and cocked her head. "I'm always careful." Then she held up her hand and silenced Christelle's listing of all their adventures so far. "I'm usually lucky."

That she was. But was it enough this time.

"Luck can be a lot." Pekoi jumped in before Christelle could shove her foot in her mouth.

Maybe she did need to calm down. Eka was a grown woman, not her child. But, if something happened to her...she couldn't handle losing anyone else. Not for a very long time, if ever.

"Just promise to be careful, even if you are lucky." Christelle preemptively wiped away the tears trying to escape her eyes.

"I promise." And Eka, who seemed to be getting more affectionate, grabbed her in a bear hug.

"Good for you, Eka." Pekoi grinned at them.

Before Eka could respond, a shimmer off to the left caught everyone's attention and Eka dropped the hug and suddenly took off towards the treeline. Christelle noticed the deep colors of Liney and smiled a bit.

"Was that the Liney person you mentioned?" Pekoi squinted at the disappearing Eka.

"Yeah."

Eka finally had someone who understood her magic, something Christelle could relate to. She was happy Eka had found a world of magic like Christelle, even there was only one other person seemed to share that world. At least Eka didn't have to have Waker groupies treating her like some wise sage, or worse, like a goddess. Like Gaia. What was wrong with them. Couldn't they see she was just a person, she hurt like everyone else.

Stop feeling sorry for yourself!

She breathed passed the jarring pain, realizing just how tired she was.

She obviously needed rest just as much as anyone else here, too bad everyone seemed to think she was invincible. And had answers to their non-stop questions. She wished her grandparents were the ones people leaned on, but they weren't available in any capacity right now.

Bu had come to take Shirley to his own community, which was apparently one of a few communities fortifying themselves with additional Wakers and devices. Christelle almost broke down when she finally found Shirley, Her grandmother, always jovial and off-beat, had looked just like Win when Sema had died, haunted and somewhere else. She couldn't even get help from her other grandparents, as Sasshine and Jan had gone with them, saying they wanted to help Shirley. But Christelle guessed they needed away from anything reminding them of Isamea.

Pekoi's arms wrapped around her from behind and she warmly floated back to the present. He really had a way of bringing her slowly back from her crazy-mind.

"You're thinking too much again." He whispered in her ear. "I have a remedy for that."

She smiled as a flash of desire instantly pushed out all her worries. But, before she could even taunt him in their usual play, an empty, cold gust blew past the group near the barn, then hit Christelle and the others. Shouting from the barn followed the gust and Christelle instinctively ran on foot toward it, Pekoi flying past and grabbing her. Even her instincts weren't Waker yet.

Next to the barn, a dark, oily portal opened and she froze.

Not yet.

This time, her fear only held her a moment before anger and protectiveness kicked in.

Out of the portal slid a man and Christelle knew the instant he stepped out, who he was. Only one person could resemble Eka is almost every way.

"Ke." Eka whispered beside Christelle, startling her, but not enough to tear her eyes from the enemy. An enemy who was right inside their camp and they were no where near ready.

"Hello Eka."

From Ke's left, a Waker sent shock waves under Ke while another Waker spun the air in an insta-tornado centered on Ke. Christelle caught her breath at their quick response, but before either attack phased him, both Wakers buckled, their attacks petering out.

He's draining both. That quick?

Beside her, Eka nodded.

But how?

She didn't get an answer for that.

All around her, Wakers stood, tension rolling off the crowd. What now?

"Eka, we can figure this out. Just come with me..." Ke gestured to her as he released the two Wakers and they lay still on the ground.

"No!" Christelle heard her shout before she knew she'd said it. Around her, murmurs floated, most of them taking a different stance. They really didn't know what Eka could do or why Ke wanted her.

Ke didn't even acknowledge the reactions, just kept smugly staring at Eka.

"Ke." Was all Eka whispered and Christelle sighed. Ke may have been her brother once but he didn't seem to even be a person any more.

A chill went up her spine as more shouting erupted in the barn. Wakers looked between Ke and the barn, some moving towards it while trying to keep him in sight.

Then a Waker erupted from the opening. "Jason's gone. Something took him!"

"Eka," Ke's voice seemed so smug now, so...confident. "You can make sure your friend is okay. What was his name, Jason?"

"*Is* Jason." Christelle didn't even give Eka time to think of an answer. "And you can bring him back right now."

"You can make sure he makes it home, Eka." Ke continued, ignoring her. "Just come with me."

Eka stood still while all around them Wakers stood just as frozen. They needed to save Jason, but Eka couldn't go, not with Lintu wanting her so bad. It had to be a setup.

"I'll go." Eka stated.

"What!" Christelle grabbed Eka. "You can't."

Eka pulled away from the crazy stand off and lowered her voice. "He can't hurt me."

"You don't know that!" Her voice was more shrill than she'd intended. Lowering it to match Eka's, she leaned toward her friend. "You don't know what they can do. Only what they've shown us."

Eka sighed. "But if he could have forced the issue, he would have."

She was right. Probably. But still, Lintu needed Eka to open that rift and let others like him through. "You can't help them."

"I won't. I just need to help Jason and any other lighters that might be there. Look," Eka leaned in, almost touching her ear, seeming to hug her, "I'll need a distraction. When Mele comes, attack their hideout." Then she sent an image of the hideout and where it was.

"What's your plan?"

"That's my plan."

Christelle hugged her friend back. "That is not a plan."

"It's more than we've ever had."

Christelle couldn't argue that, but didn't feel any confidence either.

"We don't have a choice." Eka stood back.

Just be there.

Christelle nodded, numb from this impossible situation.

Promise.

Eka nodded back, took a breath, and headed toward Ke. "I'm ready."

"Wonderful." Ke's slimy voice faded as he followed Eka into the portal and they disappeared.

Christelle Looses A Boulder

Eka stepped out of the greasy portal into air that weighed her down. She stumbled in the dark room, trying to adjust to the minimal lighting, none of which was energy. All signs of life were missing from the walls, floor, and ceiling of the cave. Then she saw Jason and half ran, half skidded over the slick rock to his body propped up against the wall.

"Jason." She bent over him, his breathing shallow but his eyes able to focus on her. "I'm getting you out of here." She barely whispered.

His uliee was faint but still flowing in him as he nodded. He lifted his hand slowly, as if gravity increased at this very spot, and he laid his hand on hers. "Eka."

How had he gotten so bad so quickly? What had they done to him? She glanced at Ke. "Why did you drain him?"

Ke held up his hands. "Someone else." He walked over to them. "But you can see he's fine."

She narrowed her eyes. "Fine?"

"He's alive. And you can make sure he gets home."

She stood, just inches from Ke's face. "Why would you do this?"

"You'll understand soon. We needed you and you wouldn't cooperate." His face softened. "Lintu has plans and needs our help. He helped us all find our strength, our own powers. Now we're not reliant on anyone. Not under them anymore."

"Ke, listen to yourself. He's hurting people."

"He's done what he had to. We all have. And now that you're here, less people need be hurt."

"Less?"

"Doesn't matter. We have to help him get his family through. They're stuck, back in his universe, where everything is dying. They need to come here, where they can thrive."

"Ke." She couldn't believe he was saying all this. "Lintu kills everything around him. If his universe is dying I bet there one reason why. And they'll destroy us if we let them in, we'll end up a dying universe too."

Ke paused a moment and frowned, then shook his head. "You have no idea what you're talking about."

"He's not your friend…"

"He's more my friend than anyone ever has been." Ke crossed his arms, setting a wall between them.

Eka reached out to Ke, then felt it. Why hadn't she noticed before, all the tainted energy flowing through him? He wasn't a Waker any more. Not only did he believe Lintu, he was part of Lintu, corrupted. Her brother was…gone.

Her hand fell and she crouched back down by Jason, holding back tears. She couldn't save him.

Ke put his hand on Eka's shoulder and she flinched away. Without missing a beat he patted her back. "I know you'll come around."

Eka stood facing him. "I'll help, but you can't hurt anyone else."

Ke nodded. "Of course."

Not much in the way of promises, but it'd have to do for now.

"Eka." Below her, Jason mumbled. "You can't do this, they won't keep any promises."

She glanced at Jason, winked, then turned and followed Ke.

Christelle hid behind a dead boulder. Eka's mental instructions to Lintu's island cave was spot on because they'd recognized the lack of energy all through the rocks surrounding the cave when they'd scouted it. Unfortunately, those freakin' military Ysians had tracked her down and were blocking the one narrow path up the cliffs to the cave. Not only were they wearing her people out, but they could accidentally alert Lintu and his minions of their presence.

How did they keep finding her and what was wrong with them? With Isamea's people?

Then she remembered Eka sharing that Sema could always keep tabs on Eka through some kind of bond. Did her mother have that with her.

Shit.

Then, her mother and her father flashed through her mind, chased by every intense emotion she'd ever felt in the last year.

Why?

A tree far off to her left disintegrated, jerking her back to the present. Her people scattered to other hiding places, trying to get some order to counter the military Ysian group. They really needed some kind of offense, but there were so unprepared.

She scanned her smaller than optimal group. There were only a few dozen, and they were so tired. But they had all agreed now was the time to make their move. Lintu already knew where the Waker hideouts were, he could have attacked, but didn't. He must be getting ready to open that end-of-the-universe rip, using Eka. So, they were out of time and needed to attack now. And she couldn't abandoned Eka to Ke. At least the groups with her had trained with the new device configuration, hopefully the communities she'd sent word to would understand her instructions on how to make and use the newly improved device and send everyone they had.

But most of all, she hoped the device worked because it was their only hope against Lintu.

A few boulders to her right disintegrated.

Damn it!

How were they ever going to get inside, if these idiots wouldn't back off. They had the same enemy, what was wrong with them?

She couldn't see any of the machines she'd seen underwater, but those assholes were draining everything around them trying to get to her group. And the only way they could do that was those freakin' machines. She really needed that device to work.

Ping! Can you see any of them?

Across from her, Ping shook his head. *They keep draining the wind but*

I'll try to get a fix.

She could hear the desperation in his mind-speak and she held back her own fears, they wouldn't help anyone right now. Especially Ping. She could see the strain in him and knew the fear and desperation he must feel with Jason captive in that cave. Worrying what Lintu, or his people, were doing to him.

What was happening to Eka.

Stop and focus. You're not helping her.

Another tree disintegrated to her right and everyone shifted again. They were running out of places to hide behind.

Why had she trusted her mom? She knew things were wrong in Ys, why hadn't she listened to her gut? Called her mom out earlier? She was so stupid!

Christelle, I think we have it! Her group's mind-voices reached her as one.

They could only be talking about the device.

Did they really have all the pieces singing? She sent them an image of where she was, hoping they could all get here and Ping could get a fix. Suddenly, the energy-less boulder she hid behind, began shaking. Energy shot out of her instinctively, engulfing the boulder, but somehow the machine was pulling it out at the same rate. No, there had to be more than one machine. How many were there, exactly? She couldn't keep sending energy to the others, who needed it for protection and healing, while staving off the machines. But, she'd worked herself into a corner. The boulder was in open ground, all other protection gone. And if she went underground, the others lost her as protection.

Damn it. Everyone up here now!

We're trying. She saw them through someone else's eyes, struggling to make it to her, jumping between what was left of the points of cover, trying not to become a target. *Are you sure you can charge this device?*

Her uliee was spread thin but she could do it if they made it to her.

Yes.

The boulder started blowing away, right under her hands. More machines had found her, now that she was exposed, and she had to redirect the rest of her uliee. Around her, more ash blew up as the little cover they had disappeared. Then, before she could respond, a Waker, not far from her, disappeared.

"No!" Christelle turned, distracted, and the pull hit her, hurting her for the first time.

She heard yelling far off in the direction of the machines and suddenly the drain started to slow. She staggered, trying to refocus and forget the disintegrating Waker, but she couldn't figure out what was happening. Somehow, the drain kept lessening. How was this possible?

"Christelle." She spun to find Isamea striding toward her. Stumbling back and holding her side, she knew she didn't have any room to redirect energy. "Get back." Christelle croaked.

Without flinching, Isamea grabbed Christelle and half pulled/half dragged her down toward the others. To the Wakers and exiled Ysians on Christelle's side. "What are you doing?"

Isamea's eyes glistened and she wrapped her arms around Christelle. "What I should have done years ago." She pushed Christelle back and looked her up and down.

"I…don't understand." Nothing made sense to Christelle, she couldn't even begin to feel anything.

Isamea shook her head, then gently brushed bits of hair out of Christelle's face.

She jerked back and a pain flashed briefly across Isamea's face.

"I know you can't forgive me." Her breath caught and her eyes unfocused. "I'll never forgive myself for what happened to him." She whispered more to herself then refocused on Christelle. "I'm sorry."

Before Christelle could even compose her thoughts, Isamea turned and headed back in the direction of the machines.

Christelle shook herself and hobbled after her, turning a corner to find Isamea jumping on a machine and battering it as she fought off the operator. The machine finally fell, next to three other broken ones. The last one turned as Isamea ran at it.

"No!" The beam hit Isamea before she could get to the machine. It must have been set high, something her mother's low uliee wasn't ready for and just like Jake, she fell.

A burst of uliee, like she'd never created before, or knew she could create, erupted from Christelle and the machine exploded, throwing the operator far off as Christelle slid next to her mom, finding herself in the same position she'd held her dad in.

"Mom." Christelle cradled her mother, trying to find the hint of uliee she could encourage. But there was so little there.

"Christelle." Isamea reached up and touched her face. "You are so grown up and I missed it all. I just wanted to protect you."

Christelle sent uliee of every type coursing through Isamea, but there was nothing that held. "Please don't go."

"I love you." As the last bit of uliee dissipated, Isamea went still.

Christelle bent over her mother's body, the fight gone out of her as she held her mom's hand. Then, a faint voice seemed to whisper to her. "I will always love you." And her mother's body disappeared.

"Mom?" She spun to find nothing but the faint impression of orange uliee.

"Christelle!" A group of Wakers ran up to her. "We've got it working."

She blinked at them, trying to make sense of them and what they were talking about. They seemed to be speaking through a fog and holding up random pieces of what? Stuff they'd found?

Ping, who was suddenly next to her, touched her palm and she looked down. Ash. Why was there ash in her hand? Ping stood her up, like she had to be positioned to move, then looked right in her eyes.

We have no time for this, if you want to save them. His voice boomed inside her, shaking her soul and grabbing her lost attention. *We will all grieve later, but now, save the ones we can.*

She nodded and suddenly, a wave of anger and hatred for that thing that had come through to their universe and destroyed so much, swept over her. She could finally focus and saw the pieces of the device and noticed her group of trainees. Everything slammed back into her memory and she took a deep breath and then saw Mele. "We've got to go."

Eka Plays With Stones And Christelle Sings A Song

E ka coughed. "Oh, sorry. Just trying to focus."

"Well, focus then." Ke scowled.

"I'm trying. I'm not sure all this is ready for…"

"He knows it's ready." Ke's voice cut her off.

"I'm not feeling it." She hedged.

"Then start feeling it!"

Her stalling was wearing thin. Where was Christelle? Had Mele made it to her?

Come on, I need that distraction guys.

"Uh, okay. I think I'm ready but…I need some water."

"Are you kidding me?" Ke narrowed his eyes but Eka just shrugged and swallowed.

"Really parched."

Ke turned to a Nalo nearby and snapped. "Get her some water." The Nalo scurried out of the chamber.

A moment later, the Nalo returned and shoved a glass of water at her.

She extracted the glass without touching the poisoned energy of the man. "Thanks. And great job on the etiquette." He just scowled, a common look around here.

"You got your water, let's do this." Ke crossed his arms.

Eka nodded and raised the glass to her lips.

Please let this be okay to drink.

Squinting, she slowly sipped the liquid, nothing weird happening. She sipped really slowly, avoiding Ke's gaze. So how long could she drag this out.

"Eka!"

About that long. She glanced at him and nodded, setting the glass down. "That was awesome. I really needed that. And boy, did you get that fast, if only restaurants were that fast…"

Ke pointed at Jason and a Nalo next to him who, suddenly sporting a big, stupid grin, started draining Jason.

"Fine! Okay, fine. I'm doing this." She looked down at the stone and felt the familiar energy. Liney's energy, her energy. She knew this was it, so she was going to have to take the chance what she was about to pull would go unnoticed. She slowly sent her energy into the stone and immediately the song started, that song of distant worlds calling her, millions of faint, beautiful songs. Flipping through them, like a music player, she reached for a very specific world and shuddered at the contact. Hopefully no one noticed what she was connected to.

Ke starred at her, and for a second she thought he caught something. Then he deepened the requisite scowl and shouted. "Focus!"

"I'm trying." She babbled, her attention split. "There are a lot of universes."

"You know the right energy, now find that damn universe!"

"You're so testy these days." She mumbled, then Jason yelled again and she looked back down at the stone. This was it, her time was up.

She found it, Lintu's universe, and she felt them pressing in. His 'family' trying desperately to get through to theirs. How did they know someone was trying to open a way through? Was he really connected to all of them, even across universes?

She took a deep breath and started to open the portal-type door in the stone's energy. This was it. Greasy shadows were slithering around, starting to bulge through. And just when she couldn't figure out how to pull out her bag of stone bits without anyone seeing, especially Ke, an explosion rocked the cave. Yelling erupted all around her as the solid walls shook briefly. Next to her, Ke stumbled and at that moment she grabbed the bag, opened it and put the rocks down behind her, then focused. She'd never opened two portals at the same time. Now she was opening two multi-universe portals and with broken stones.

She took a deep breath and searched. And found it easier this time, but the shiver was worse.

"Eka! What are you doing?" Ke shouted and she glanced briefly at him, dropping her focus. The portals sputtered as Ke ran at her.

Christelle ran around the side of the rock face, blocking the energy that was being sucked away from it by adding her own. Images of her mother, fighting all those Ysian, just to help her, threatened to send her over the edge just at the wrong moment. Then, Tine came up behind her, and the rest of her small group joined while others still hid across the landscape. Every single one of Tine's group was scared and freaked out and looking to Christelle for any direction that might make this better.

Get it together!

She refocused just as her group started to move into the device configuration and she was able to stop them. "Not the device, just get ready!"

"Are you kidding? How're we getting past them without using the only weapon we have?"

Christelle shook her head. "Trust me, the recharge would take too long and these Nalos are easy compared to Lintu. We'll figure it out." They had to, Eka needed help. But they had already lost a few members and were now in a stalemate with these Nalos, just like at the orange factory in Manatee Isles and back in dying Ys.

Wait, Ys. Then she remembered.

"Okay, this is what we're doing." Christelle gathered the others closest to her as she sent energy deep underground, past the Nalos, and up behind and sputtered out as there was no energy in it to react. It was dead.

Shit.

"What're you trying to do?" Tine asked, confusion reflected in the groups' faces.

"If I can get those rocks to move just right, I can knock out the Nalos." It was so simple and so impossible.

The group immediately went into brain storm mode, Christelle's exhausted mind and spirit barely holding on, let alone really hearing to the ideas pouring in.

"Christelle!" Tine nudged her shoulder.

"Huh?" She refocused on the group, all huddle behind the boulder she was feeding.

Tine rolled her eyes. "Can we use a breeze to pick up the rock?"

Christelle peaked around the boulder and observed how all spirits ending up in the Nalo's area were drained and now all of them avoided the whole space. In fact, there hadn't been any breeze or animals for the last half mile. She turned back to Tine and shook her head. "There's no air spirit that'll go over there."

"Didn't you say the device wasn't just a weapon?" Klain frowned, seeming to try and remember what she'd said. "That it was a, uh, alive?"

"Yeeeaaah." Christelle wasn't sure where he was going with this.

"Well, you gave us more energy, an upgrade, so maybe the device, with so much energy, can reinvigorate those stones."

"That's an interesting theory." And it really was. "But I had energy to work with in each of you. And we won't have time to recharge it."

"Oh." Klain sagged.

"But." Tine spoke up, face scrunched up in thought. "What if it could bring back the rock, it is like Gaia, you said. And what if we didn't need the most energy, just some. We might not need to recharge it that much."

"I never said it was like Gaia." Christelle blurted out, in her foggy brain she was really having trouble focusing. Then, from behind her, a whole strand of trees suddenly disintegrated and with them two more of the Wakers she'd brought. Two more barely grown people who had followed her, trusted her to bring them back in one piece. And with those bodies went the entire mood of Tine's group, she could feel them giving up before her. At that moment she realized they didn't have a choice any more, she had to try anything or they would all die here, before they had a chance at Lintu and stopping the opening to that other freakin universe.

"Okay, let's try this." The group looked around at each other and she could almost feel the mood lift with that little bit of direction and hope. "But remember, you're part of the device, so don't drain yourselves too much."

The group gathered, dirt and grime covering every inch of their bodies and faces, while they wore exhaustion like a heavy coat. But despite the lack of sleep and wariness, they each held their piece of Gaia and focused. Tine started, gently sending her own uliee into the ocean rock she'd carried from her exiled home underwater. Her energy sang and the rock's energy unfurled at a snails pace, as rocks are want to do, and sang it's own song as it wound with Tine's energy, until they were vibrating at a single frequency and…singing a single, new song. Christelle had seen this before, in practice, but it had always fell apart within seconds. Maybe in her tiredness, her inability to be tense and worry any longer, Tine was letting go and just existing with the rock. Whatever the reason, the melded energy suddenly erupted with bits of gold and silver flakes floating through the brown as the new song emerged. The song floated over to Klain as he brought fire out of the oil container he held and sang to it until a new song grew out of their entwined energies and joined Tine's to create a slightly richer tone. One by one, each member of the group created a note to add to this song that only those in tune with the energies of Gaia could hear, or maybe feel, because it wasn't Christelle's ears catching all this, but her body. As the last member joined the energy orchestra, Tine led a shift in the tempo which shifted the music from around them to down in the earth. Christelle watched as the energy, or really the song, plunged through the dead earth and zipped down, headed for the rocky wall behind the Nalos. She dropped next to where it had entered the ground and placed her hands on it. And gasped. Everywhere the song touched, she felt life growing, the ground coming back to life. Creation.

"No way." She whispered to herself a feeling of possibilities and wonder filling her with the contact.

She broke contact and caught her breath as the uplifting feeling emptied out of her and a sudden weight back in place. Forcing herself to turn and peak around the boulder, she realized the Nalos had taken a break from draining everything around them. She wasn't sure why, but was happy they and hopefully they didn't have any of the Ys' draining machines. At the thought of the machines, she sank as her mother's and father's death rushed back into her memory. She'd never see them again, watch storms roll in with her dad from their trailer, create new memories with her mother. Her body sank down, gravity overwhelming her. How would she ever breath again.

Suddenly, a roar, which could only come from a spirit, went through the whole area and threw her attention back to the present. She blinked and scanned, her group somehow still focused on their singing. She glanced around the boulder as voices erupted in shouts and screams. Out of the wall, an earth spirit rose up…out of a previously dead rock.

Wait, the rock now wasn't dead any more and it seethed with energy. How?

Christelle glanced back at her group then down where the song entered the ground. It literally glowed with its own energy.

Holy crap!

She looked back toward the Nalo group and saw them scrambling away from the spirit. Had they killed it when they drained the rock or had it gone into hibernation or something else? Was it even the original spirit? Whatever the answers to those questions were, it was well and truly pissed off. And, as the Nalo tried to drain the area again, using the only weapon they had, the song kept feeding the spirit, somehow reinvigorating everything the Nalo's extracted. But the spirit had it's own weapon and as the Nalo backed up, the spirit broke off chunks of rock that could have covered a large house and hurled them, leaving no doubt to the fate of the fleeing Nalo. Christelle caught her breath as a Nalo came screaming by their group and realized a car sized rock was headed their way. Guess the spirit wasn't too discriminating.

In a split second, she threw her energy away from the boulder she hid behind and into the ground, calling on the newly energized earth to sink the group down. In the blink of any eye, the earth dropped under each member of the group, breaking the song of the dazed participants just as the rock bounced off the area they'd stood in, and bounced a few more times, one of them over the fleeing Nalo.

Near the wall, with the song gone, the spirit wasn't as protected, but it no longer needed protection as it's mission was successful. Christelle watched as the subdued spirit sank back into the newly renewed rock.

"Christelle!" Tine shouted from her hole as she scrambled out. "What happened? Did it work?"

The others slowly emerged from their own holes and Christelle joined them as all the other remaining Wakers from their original group staggered up.

She stared at the core device group and smiled wearily. "You did it. And," she took a deep breath, barely believing it herself, "you brought the rock and spirit back to life."

"What happened?" They all seemed to ask at once. And they were greeted with by recounts by the various Wakers who were part of the whole thing.

Christelle, we're coming with back up. Eiriol's voice reached her and the half-filled mission ploughed into her awareness.

"Everyone, I know how beyond amazing that was, but there's still the rest of the mission to finish."

Klain spoke up just then. "I hate to bring this up, but I think I'm drained." Murmurs from the rest of the device group confirmed they all were.

Christelle sighed, she had no idea how long they would need before they could create the device again. And they really needed it. "I'll try and recharge you as we go." She looked at the group. "And anyone here that I upgraded, try and help with the recharge. We have more Wakers coming and they might have their own groups that can create the device." She turned to Tine and the others. "If there are any others, help them understand what they need to do."

Tine nodded.

"Okay, we've probably lost the advantage of surprise so take a few minutes and regroup. We're going in as soon as the others get here."

The larger contingent nodded, almost in resignation. And she didn't blame them, they were going in without the advantage of surprise or the device.

Eka got the portals under control just as Ke tried to grab her. She dodged him, almost losing focus again and then he headed straight for Jason. Her uliee already strained, she managed to portal Jason out of the caves and to somewhere outside, just as Ke tried to drain him. Unfortunately, her stone pieces dropped and that needed world slipped away. She tried to stop the door from the other stone portal, but she'd let it get too far. They were coming through. Eka dropped to the ground and grabbed at the broken stones.

"Eka!" Christelle broke into the chamber followed by dozens of others. Around her, a small group clustered and Eka swore she could hear some kind of faint song fading in and out of the energy in their hands.

Eka grabbed as many stone pieces as she could and ran. Behind her, shadows were slipping through an impossible opening in the air. An opening that tore into another universe. She couldn't look, she had to focus.

Then, all around them, inky, oily energy started seeping through the walls. And the voice was there. *Welcome.*

Lintu.

Damnit.

Christelle and her group were cornered now, fighting both the Nalos in the chamber and the shadows that had managed to push though. The Nalos didn't even realize yet that these shadows, the ones they thought were on their side, were emptying them of uliee. Soon they'd all be overwhelmed because Eka knew, in her uliee, there were thousands more of those oily shadows pushing to get through that damn opening.

Distracted by all of it, Eka fell as Ke knocked her down. The pieces scattered from her hand, but instead of hitting the ground, they floated lightly around Ke, stopping midair behind him. And somehow, he hadn't noticed.

"You're too late Eka. Just quit." Ke shook his head as the Nalos, now low in number, began to realize what was happening to them.

Unfortunately, there were few of them and Christelle's group were being herded into a tightening corner. Eka noticed Christelle's energy was becoming thin, trying to protect her teammates whose energy was dangerously low. With Christelle getting weaker so they were left fighting hand to hand, while a few of the Nalo's were still trying to drain them.

Christelle's group huddled together, some Wakers physically fighting Nalos as she dumped energy into the device group and they kept trying to reignite the song while using more of her energy to block the Nalos or Shadows from draining any Wakers.

"Get them singing together!" Christelle nearly yelled, except her teeth were gritted.

"We're trying!" A few yelled back.

Around them, shadows were closing in while Lintu oozed from the walls. Oozed! The body that had held it was gone, it was pure…whatever that stuff was.

"No!" Tine shivered next to Christelle as the rest of her teammates froze. Lintu, or the oily ooze that was Lintu, flowed over a Nalo and the person just disappeared.

Consumed.

Christelle's whole body sank into her stomach and it churned. But it was Tine who threw up. Well, her and a few others.

Christelle spun on the frozen group and slapped each and every one of them.

"Hey!"

"What the hell?"

"Ouch." Tine rubbed her cheek, shock in her eyes.

"Focus on me." Christelle strained to keep the energy flowing against the onslaught, their group retreating toward the back wall, where ooze continued to pore out. How much of it was there? All around them, it rolled in and she wasn't sure how to stop this. It's like the shadows were merging together, forming that gunk. But their group needed to focus if there was going to be even a chance.

"Sing with me." She took a breath and hummed, trying to sound like the calm in the storm.

"What?" The group just stared at her.

Until the pieces vibrated a bit in tune.

"Try." She breathed out the word, still humming.

Then, little by little, they turned away from the encroaching oiliness, lifted their hands with all the small mundane pieces, and sang.

Eka found it again. That universe she'd opened before. She gritted her teeth but held onto it, keeping it on the other side of the portal as cold seeped into her.

Ke knelt next to her, fortunately oblivious to the universe opening behind him. "We can be a family again. With him. You have to see."

"Ke, can't you see?" She knew it was futile, but she needed the time. "Look around you. He's killing them all."

But Ke ignored the request as his eyes clouded over in dark grey, a grey haziness that was sinking into his body. She watched in horror, finally turning to trace the haze. It was Lintu, or the shadow that was Lintu, and it was taking over her brother, using his body.

Then, Ke's Gaian uliee, or energy, was gone and Lintu's shadow or whatever it was, had subsumed Ke. He was part of the shadows now.

"You can be with us, Eka."

Her brother wasn't there, it was Lintu in Ke's face. Controlling him. Or Ke was Lintu now. She wasn't sure of any of this but she knew there was only the one chance to stop this monster.

But would it work?

A faint song, building up and amplifying itself, drifted into her awareness. She glanced over as Christelle's group, now surrounded by the oiliness of Lintu, sang. And that song was building from them, larger then them. Their Uliee were collectively transforming into the most intense pulse of…life she'd ever felt. It went through her, buoyed her. She suddenly had hope. Not the hope she'd wanted, but hope for the others, if she could do this.

Ke/Lintu's face, now staring at Christelle's group, look famished. As if he hadn't eaten in an entire lifetime.

Christelle.

She wasn't sure she'd gotten through with the whisper but she needed to try.

Eka?

They're eyes met, Christelle holding a whole world's hope. This friend, who couldn't even voice her opinion when they'd first met, was now the most powerful Gaian in the Waker world. This friend who'd argued that she'd never work with Wakers, let alone lead them, was leading a group of newbies against an other universe, energy sucking monster. And why? To bring to life an experimental being that might be the only chance they had of destroying this creature.

You're doing it.

Christelle strained.

We need more time.

Eka nodded. Her brother stood over her, now oblivious to her because he could only see the energy Christelle's group was putting out. His body pulsed for it and her gut knew this wasn't Ke's body anymore. It was Lintu's.

I've got it. And you're the best friend I've ever had. I love ya.

Christelle's frown deepened. *Eka?*

Eka turned to Ke, as her tears were unleashed. While he was distracted, she sent a message to Mele. Then, as he stared at the small group who sang a song of life and hope, she stood, wrapped him in a hug, and buried her head in his shoulder. "I love you Ke." Then she portaled them into the door to that cold, empty universe.

As they fell into that universe, she glanced at the tiny, disappearing figure of Christelle, saw her yelling but couldn't hear it as they fell further in. Then this dead, cold universe started pulling at them. Lintu/Ke's shadow energy was strong, but not strong enough for this. She could have sworn he was screaming but couldn't hear him anymore, or feel the struggle.

"Eka!" Christelle screamed. Where was she? Why had she disappeared with Ke? What was that rip they fell into?

Energy like Eka's streaked past her and she turned to find Mele picking up the unbroken stone and flinging it at the wall. The shattering rumbled through the entire chamber and at that moment, the opening that had let in Lintu's people, that still had shadows pushing through, broke apart, shattering the last shadows into a million hazy bits with a guttural screech. Christelle knew this was important but her heart sank as she finally let herself realize what had happened to Eka.

From seemingly far off, Christelle's name seeped into her awareness. A few blinks later, she saw her group still singing. Then, around her, the oiliness began to look different. It seemed to be shriveling up. The Ysian fighters were attacking it and…winning.

The song. "It's working?"

The group nodded and Christelle inhaled deeply. Eka'd done it, she'd weakened it! But the flash of Eka falling into that tear crushed her happiness. "Oh Eka. Where are you?" But the question was more about willful denial then ignorance.

Eka? The weak mindspeak brushed against her mind and she stiffened.

Ke?

Lifting her energy form away from his shoulder, she saw the real Ke in his eyes. *Thank you. For saving me.*

You. Your here!

Her brother was alive!

We need to get back. You need help.

Her thoughts spun and she concentrated on opening a portal, a rift. But there were no rocks, nothing to guide her out of this unknown place. Eka's mind and heart sunk. What had she done?

I killed you.

He shook his head. *He's still in me.* Ke coughed. *He won't let go.*

A freezing hand touched her hazy face. *You set me free. I love you.*

Then, his body slumped and his head rolled back, the last of the oiliness dissipating from him. And his body drifted away from her, slowly dissolving.

I love you forever.

Her own uliee had transformed her into pure energy, but she wouldn't last forever. Not here, where there was now truly no other life. But she didn't care, not anymore.

The shadows that had come through hadn't had time to build up strength in this universe and without Lintu to protect them, their attacks were easily overpowered. Christelle's group moved through the room, destroying the weakened shadows that hid away from them. The device group was running low on uliee, but, with only a little energy, zap, they were dust. And the few Wakers and exiled Ysians that were left, were rounding up the Nalos.

But Eka was still gone.

A zip of color, the color of deep space, spun up around some stone pieces.

Liney!

As the deep space energy settled on the pieces, a haziness developed above them. Flashes of different spaces spun through the haze, like a wheel spinning, until it stopped moving, seeming to land on a bit of cold, pitch black emptiness. And Liney's energy was stretching right into it.

Eka.

The voice sounded so faint, like the echo of someone she knew. She couldn't look around, she didn't have a head and, besides, there wasn't anything to look at. Maybe leftover sounds were part of dying this way. She really couldn't tell.

And maybe that flash of uliee, so familiar, was part of it too.

Wake up, not time for you to go.

Suddenly, the uliee wrapped around her and…pulled. She did something that felt like a blink and knew it was Liney.

Liney!

Yes it is me.

But how?

I can sing the songs. And Eka swore there was a smile in that mindspeak, right before she fell through a portal and back into the cave, collapsing into a solid form.

Liney floated over her, smiling. Eka had always laughed when she'd faced that floating head sitting on pure uliee. This time, a sputtering laugh erupted from her carrying a lifetime of emotions she wouldn't acknowledge. Yet.

Exhausted, she scanned the cave. Everything around her was in shambles, but Christelle was still there limping toward her. And others, cleaning up the shadows and Nalo. The exhaustion accelerated and, before Christelle reached her, the world went blank.

Epilogue

Beyond The Rainbow

The barn stood, more sturdy these days. The land around them, now the main Waker community, seemed much more inviting than it ever had. Above, Eka air surfed against Christelle, only winning when she portalling ahead.

"Hey!" Christelle yelled and Eka barrel rolled, laughing as they flew around the airship, which was moored above the barn.

After too many loops to count, Eka flew into the rigging, grabbing a vine and swinging around it. "Now this is exactly what I needed!" She swung around it again as Christelle slid in next to her. "About time you caught up, Queen of the Wakers."

"I'm not a queen!" Christelle almost flew backwards as wind picked up around them, sails flapping wildly.

"Hey." Eka laughed, hands up in surrender. "Just a joke."

Christelle's face slowly lost its pink shade, her body and uliee relaxing. "Yeah."

Eka elbowed Christelle. "Enjoy all this. Wakers traveling more and learning from each other. This new community that's practically the center of everything Waker. All because of you." She winked at Christelle. "You're quite persuasive with all this Gaian upgrade."

"I guess. But it's a lot of work. Every single problem is something they think I can solve. I'm only in my twenties, not fifties."

"Or hundreds."

"Right!" Christelle shook her head. "I just learned how to get the Ysians to let other Wakers into the new Ys. And that's only because I promised to help rebuild."

"Pretty smooth negotiation tactic." Eka nodded while raising her eyebrows.

Christelle rolled her eyes. "I can't do that with everyone. Nothing would ever get built waiting for me!" Her voice rose a little at the end there.

"Hey." Eka slid her board over to Christelle's puff of air and wrapped her arm around her neck. "Look at all those Wakers." She pointed below them, to the bustling community building mound homes out of the grass. "Not sure I'd want to live in those, but they do blend in."

"Kinda confining." Christelle nodded.

"Never thought that barn would be the center of everything."

"They really needed a big place to put all that Asleep tech."

Eka glanced at Christelle. "I totally believe in your non-queen leadership abilities with this lot, you know that right?"

Christelle sighed. "I know, thinking of connecting with the Asleep is beyond crazy. But Gaia insisted we have to make an alliance or there might be another war." Her hands clinched. "I don't think I have that in me, a war with the Asleep."

Eka's sigh sank after Christelle's. "I get it. Why are humans so irritable. And opinionated. And…"

"Ready to fight over anything?"

"Yep." Eka nodded. "I don't envy your job at all. And being a woman…"

"A young woman."

"That too. Getting the Asleep to take you seriously is gonna take all the Gaia juice you have."

They both sighed together this time.

"I suppose it's unavoidable that the Asleep would figure out we're here, after the mess Lintu left." Christelle sank into the rigging, Eka following.

"I miss New Mexico with the vardo." Eka stated into the quiet. "No one to bother us, just sunrises and sunsets."

"Except Win."

"And Shirley and Bu."

"And Sashine and Jan."

"And Pekoi. But he kinda lived there after a while."

Christelle nodded, a small smile creeping across his face. "I don't think I could have faced anyone else during those months."

Eka nodded agreement and neither one of them mentioned the months of barely breathing or of crying and staring at walls.

"Six months away was good, but I did kinda missed my magic." Eka smiled at her friend. "You know you missed it too."

Christelle nodded. "Yeah, but I just wasn't ready."

"Yeah."

They both examined the night sky, looking at stars they'd grown familiar with during their hiatus from the Waker world.

"Amazing how chaotic the Wakers let everything get." Eka mumbled.

"Right?" Christelle sat up. "I can't believe they still tried to stick to their own communities, after everything."

"Good thing they had you." Eka nudged Christelle and she blushed.

"I didn't do much."

This time Eka rolled her eyes. "You my friend need to get over your modesty hangup. You practically forced them to build this center and create those exchange programs. And it didn't take more than a year for them to embrace it. I do think A'he is your biggest fan though."

"Maybe, but I'm not the only one who made big changes." Christelle half smiled at Eka. "But I really wish you were staying. I could use your support."

"You're gonna do great!" Eka nudged Christelle again. "You've got Pekoi. And Shirley and Sashine will never leave you alone, knowing those two." Eka winked.

"Yeah, I'm really glad they're coming out here for a while to help get this main community running. And Jan and Bu promised to drop by on their travels."

"I can't believe they have a common interest in birding. Who would've guessed that?"

"Right?" Chritselle shook her head. "So, have you seen Win since New Mexico?"

Eka sagged just a bit. "No. Eiriol and Yang are sticking with him. They say he's doing better but I think it's going to be a few more years. Sema was his rock."

"Yeah."

Again, a familiar quiet, born in their New Mexico hideaway, settled over them, as insect songs drifted over the sound of people below.

And as usual, Eka was the first to break the silence.

"Can you believe how big Brigg is getting?" Eka laughed. "And how much of a helicopter parent Ping is?"

"He's totally wrapped around her finger." Christelle put her hand on Eka shoulder. "You know he almost ended up like Win, he almost lost it when Jason was in that cave. You really saved both their lives."

Eka nodded and of course, changed the subject. "So, you and Pekoi, parents, huh?"

Christelle, finally comfortable with Eka's redirects, slapped her shoulder. "I don't know how you always know things before I tell you." She smiled at Eka. "I was going to tell you before you left. It's twins."

"That's awesome! And remember, Ekanam is a great name."

Christelle rolled her eyes, but laughed. "I'm so gonna miss you."

"You'll be fine. Shirly and Sashine will make sure everyone falls in line. Besides, I still don't fit here, even if Lintu is gone."

"We could get them used to you. To understand better."

Eka shook her head. "That's too much work and too little fun. Besides, seems some of the lighters are starting to warm to me and some are even itching to check out those other universes with me and Liney." Eka laughed. "I can't believe I just said that."

Christelle shook her head. "I can't believe a lot of things. Like how lighters are related to whoever came through those portals."

"Liney said the stories she'd heard from her people probably mean they came through. But she also said there are other people out there in that vastness, and I think it's time we found out who they are. I'll tell you, I think Liney's ready to not hide from Wakers anymore, and so am I."

Christelle nodded while looking her right in the eyes. "Just promise to be a tiny bit careful."

"Promise." And there was finally a bit of seriousness in Eka's answer.

"Oh." Eka broke that awkwardness. "Thanks for taking care of my home."

Christelle smiled. "Pekoi loves driving the truck. He's never driven anything, let along a stick shift and I think he only got stuck twice yesterday."

Eka winced. "Don't tell me anything else and I'll dream of smooth highways and no potholes."

Christelle finally laughed.

Below them, a single Waker with little uliee, walked ahead of a group of Wakers toward a large mound. A military Ysian.

"I wish they'd all chosen to stay Wakers. Why would they want their memories wiped, their gifts gone?"

Eka shook her head. "Guess they couldn't handle what they did. At least it's a choice."

"Yeah."

A number of Wakers were shouting up at Eka.

"Well, sounds like my group is waiting."

"Already? I thought we had a few more days." Christelle's face scrunched quickly.

"We've been planning for a month and the portals are singing so loud I'm surprised all these Wakers can't hear them."

"I finally hear them." Christelle answered wistfully. "And I don't blame you, it's a beautiful song. But I'll miss you."

"Me too."

They floated toward a swirling, flashing spot way behind the barn and landed in a group of lighters. The rest of the community seemed to be gathering in a circle around them.

Curiosity sometimes overcame fear.

Christelle and Eka looked at each other.

"Don't let them ever tell you you're not in charge, okay?" Eka half grinned, half teared up.

Christelle shook her head. "And don't do anything we wouldn't do." She wiped away a tear. "Not even half of what we would do."

Eka swiped at an escaped tear. "Promise." And she held up crossed fingers as they fell into a hug.

"Okay." Eka stepped out of the hug and took a breath. "Here comes adventure." Mele crashed into her arm as Fluffy swirled around them. Eka petted Fluffy as much as an air spirit can be petted and Mele chittered to her.

"Yeah, we'll miss you too." Eka leaned in. "Take care of those two." She nodded at Christelle as Pekoi joined the group, wrapping his arms around Christelle.

Fluffy swirled in agreement then breezed over to Pekoi as Eka smiled, maybe a little sadly. Until a deep energy zipped next to her and solidified into Liney.

Can we go now?

"Of course." Eka grinned and turned to the group of lighters that were joining them. They were only a few, but they seemed to have the most otherworld energy running through them, so Eka and Liney had worked with them to bring out any non-Gaian magic. They may still need shields to survive in space but some of them were already showing surprising abilities to morph small objects.

"I guess that's it then." She turned to the send off group, mostly people who had been walking by, and gave a grand wave before almost being bowled over by Christelle in a bear hug. Eka sank into the hug and squeezed back for a long while.

"Do not get yourself killed." Christelle's muffled voice barely made it to Eka's ears.

"I promise."

Christelle finally pulled herself away and wiped yet another tear away. "We've had a heck of a journey."

"No kidding."

"Just," she rubbed her nose, "stay safe." She turned to Liney. "You too."

Yes, yes. We go now.

Eka and Christelle exchanged giggles then burst out laughing.

Eka nodded, catching her breath, and gave Pekoi a wave then squeezed Christelle's shoulder before spinning around and walking to this newly refurbished stone's portal, already opened by Liney.

Just before she disappeared completely, she glanced back at Christelle and Pekoi. "Better get going before I can't"

And, as Liney dematerialized and rushed through, Eka took another deep breath as Mele settled into her arm and stepped into the unknown.

Eka and Christelle's journey has ended, for now. To know when their next adventure starts, or adventures of other quirky characters, signup to get alerts at **DreamingOfDancingBubbles.com**

Until next time, wonderful travels!

www.ingramcontent.com/pod-product-compliance
Lightning Source LLC
Chambersburg PA
CBHW020038310726

48970CB00007B/2312